My Estranged Lover

Middlemarch Shifters 5

Shelley Munro

My Estranged Lover

Print ISBN: 978-1-99-106305-2
Digital ISBN: 978-0-473-35576-0

Editor: Mary Moran

Cover: Kim Killion, Killion Group Inc.

This book is a work of fiction. The names, characters, places, and incidents are products of the writer's imagination or have been used fictitiously and are not to be construed as real. Any resemblance to persons, living or dead, actual events, locales, or organizations is entirely coincidental.

Munro Press, New Zealand.

First Munro Press electronic publication May 2016

First Munro Press print publication November 2022

For Paul.

Introduction

Mistakes are easy. It's fixing them that can make or break a marriage.

Caroline Rutherford is at the end of her marriage tether. As much as she loves her husband, it's time to admit defeat. Their long-term, love-at-first-sight relationship is no longer working, and they're hurting each other and their two young sons by continuing the happy family farce.

Feline shifter Marsh Rutherford knows his relationship is in trouble, and he and Caroline, his human wife, haven't shared a bed for months. He made a mistake at the start of their marriage, omitting to tell the truth, and now the secrets are strangling their happiness. Admitting the reality to himself is simple, but finding a solution to fix the problem is tearing him apart because reality has the potential to destroy what little trust remains between him and his wife.

Their future looks murky until a new opportunity presents

itself—a fresh start for the entire family, a means for husband and wife to reconnect in and out of the bedroom. Caroline and Marsh agree to grasp the chance for a new future. Things are going well and their sex life has never been better, but those mysterious secrets hover in the background like pesky flies. Marsh must discover a way to make everything right because Caroline is his mate and the only woman who can make him happy. Losing her isn't an option.

Warning: contains a sexy feline shapeshifter felled by a good woman. He's confused and befuddled and makes mistakes, but it's not too late, folks. We can fix this mess with love, with tears and a few humorous mishaps during the romantic journey. Fingers crossed...let's go!

Chapter 1

A Broken Marriage

Caroline Rutherford reclined in her double bed and stared at the pages of her romance novel, despite the lateness of the hour. Instead of following the raven-haired Scottish lass as she led her hunky Highlander on an adventurous dance, her mind kept sliding to her own life.

Where was Marsh?

Out again.

With another woman if her mother-in-law's barbed hints held truth.

She hadn't summoned the courage to ask Marsh.

Yet.

Sighing, she shut the book and set it aside. Caroline rearranged her pillows and flicked off the light, plunging the bedroom into darkness.

With sight obscured, her other senses worked harder. The tick of the alarm clock sprang into focus, beating off the seconds, the minutes, the hours her husband stayed away from the house. The nights he slept in the spare bed. She sucked in a breath and caught a whiff of laundry powder, a trace of cinnamon from the candle she'd burned earlier, the spicy hint of her green tea perfume.

With a trace of embarrassment at her weakness, she reached beneath the pillow on the other side of the bed and pulled out a T-shirt—one of Marsh's. She'd behaved like a stalker to get this, stealing her husband's favorite T-shirt from the laundry hamper. Her throat tightened even as his comforting scent wrapped around her senses.

Tears stung her eyes as the truth loomed in her mind.

It was time.

Their marriage couldn't continue in this fashion, not if she wanted to retain her sanity.

A vehicle pulled up outside the house—one of the farmhouses reserved for workers. At least she'd won that argument and insisted they have their own home instead of moving into the large Rutherford homestead. Caroline's stomach rolled, the knots twisting, turning, tightening until she wanted to scream in frustration.

But she remained silent.

She froze, tension in every muscle, in every slow, even breath.

The back door squealed open, squealed shut.

Her hands curled to fists.

The old wooden floorboards creaked under the weight of footsteps.

Her fingernails dug into her palms.

Another door squeaked, softer with less of a protest.

The grip around her heart softened, emotion spilling a tear free.

Marsh was checking on Ricky. No matter how wide the gap yawned between them, she knew he loved their two boys, which made this situation even more difficult.

The door squeaked again. Footsteps neared their bedroom, stilled outside the ajar door.

Caroline's breath caught, held. Sharp teeth bit into her bottom lip.

The pause lengthened.

Her heart hammered.

Then the measured footsteps resumed, the creaks retreating as Marsh walked to the bedroom at the far end of the passage.

Maybe he was checking on James. Maybe he'd return.

She waited and waited and waited.

Marsh didn't make a return trip, choosing to sleep in the spare bed in James's room instead of sleeping with her. A long-standing habit.

Tears slid down her cheeks, one after the other.

She couldn't go on this way.

She'd talk to Marsh.

Tomorrow.

· ❤ · ❤ · ❤ · ❤ · ❤ ·

T he early morning light struck his face, and Marsh groaned. Every muscle ached and his cheek—grazed by an exuberant tackle during the madcap rugby game the previous night and still tender—stuck to his pillow. Despite his feline genes and ability to heal fast, he felt like a flat tire. He peeled the cotton from his face and rolled over to see his oldest son staring at him from the twin single bed.

"Hey, sport," Marsh whispered. "You're awake early."

James crinkled his nose, his action reminding Marsh of Caroline. "You were making noises."

"Me?"

"Yeah. Like this." James wrinkled his button nose again and let out several loud snorts.

"I made those noises?" Snoring. He shouldn't have stayed for two beers after the run with his friends. He'd known it, but he'd enjoyed being himself, embracing his feline form without worrying Caroline might discover his secret.

Marsh slid from the bed and stood, stretching with caution as he tested his limbs. Not too bad. He turned to his son and smiled. "Go back to sleep, huh?" Marsh stooped to tuck the covers around his son's slight form. Although James took after him in appearance, Marsh saw so much of Caroline in his five-year-old son. Another topic of conflict with his parents.

Marsh drew back with a sigh and left the bedroom, pulling the door closed before heading to the kitchen. Coffee. Caffeine to clear his head and give him divine inspiration. He needed it.

His marriage was dying.

Oh, he could blame his parents for the way they belittled Caroline behind her back. He could blame them for giving him advice that had placed his marriage in danger. He could blame them for rejecting the human he'd introduced to the Rutherford family.

Marsh swiped a hand through his hair and admitted the truth. The mess his marriage had become was all on him. He'd been the one who had listened to his horrified parents in the early days of his marriage. He'd been the one who agreed to conceal their feline shapeshifter heritage. He'd been the one who kept feline secrets and business from his wife.

Damn it. He'd kept himself from marking Caroline and making her his mate and wife in truth.

Marsh made the coffee, doing the mundane actions by rote. A noise from behind had him whirling to face the doorway. Caroline stood there, looking as exhausted as he felt.

Strawberry-blonde hair lay in waves, long enough to reach her shoulders. Tall and always big-boned, two pregnancies had added to her curves and size. She was beautiful, and still did it for him, even though his mother derided Caroline for her lack of willpower with food. Her light blue eyes appeared wary and he forced a smile, forced himself not to drag her into his arms. Sex obscured the problem, made it worse.

7

"Coffee?"

"Please," she said, her gaze scurrying over his bare chest, flitting to his boxer-briefs then darting to his face and settling on his grazed cheek.

Marsh willed his body not to react to her presence. Thought of cold showers and decided to flee and regroup. "Coffee won't be long. I'll grab clothes." He strode from the kitchen and turned toward their bedroom—Caroline's bedroom now. Somehow, they'd fallen into the routine of him sleeping elsewhere. Either on the couch or the spare bed in James's bedroom.

Hell, this couldn't continue.

He needed to grow a pair and fix this.

Marsh grabbed a pair of worn jeans from the wardrobe and pulled on a black T-shirt before returning to the kitchen. Caroline sat at the scarred kitchen table, a mug of coffee cupped in her hands. James's green lunch box sat on the counter. Several colorful pots filled with herbs jostled for space on the window ledge.

Everything in the kitchen screamed old and well-worn. No dishwasher. No slick cabinets. No gadgets. Yet despite this, Caroline had made the kitchen, the entire house scream welcome. It was the haven and home he'd never had while growing up. His parents' house, ten minutes down the road, seemed stiff and formal in comparison.

No, Caroline didn't deserve this crap.

It was up to him to fix this wreck of a marriage because Caroline had tried. She'd tried so hard.

Marsh reached for a mug and poured a black coffee. "Do you want a refill?"

"No, thanks."

God, so polite.

Marsh pulled out the wooden chair opposite Caroline and sat.

"What happened to your face?"

"I went to rugby training last night. Felix Mitchell tackled me hard and I'm wearing the marks to prove it."

"I didn't think you had time to play rugby this season. Your father said he couldn't spare you on the farm."

His father didn't want to pay wages and preferred the slave labor provided by his son. "I'm playing." He lifted his gaze from his coffee. "As long as you're okay with me spending a couple of nights a week training and playing on Saturday. I can take the boys with me during the early training night because a lot of the wives bring the kids and organize games in the school hall. Or, you can come to training too. It's up to you."

Marsh caught her surprise, the slight widening of her blue eyes, the wrinkling of her nose and the parting of her pink lips. Then, she tensed, her mouth firming, her spine hitting the back of the chair.

"We need to talk, Marsh."

Marsh nodded.

"We...I can't go on like this. I—it's soul-destroying."

Marsh came to a quick decision. Nothing important on his schedule today. He had to shift the cattle closer to the yards since they were selling a hundred head at the Wednesday sale, make sure they had water. "I have to shift the cattle, but why don't we spend the rest of the day together? Go for a walk on the beach or have lunch in Dunedin."

Caroline gestured at the pile of mail on the far corner of the table. "We can't afford a lunch."

Bills. Marsh glanced at his coffee, feeling worse than ever. His father seemed to think he should work for free and grudged every cent he paid in minimum wages. The reason he'd suggesting selling part of their herd. He'd told his father they didn't have enough feed to winter them, which was true. "Maybe we could—"

The landline rang, and Marsh sighed. He reached over and plucked the hand piece from the charger. "Marsh, when are you going to shift the cattle?"

"As soon as I've had my coffee." He glanced at his watch. Almost eight. Early even for his father.

"Lots to do today. Once you've mustered the cattle, I need you to mend the fence in the western paddock. I've got the wire and staples in the shed."

"Not today, Dad. After I've shifted the cattle, I'm taking off the rest of the day."

Pregnant silence bloomed. "Why?"

"I haven't had a day off for weeks."

"But what about the fence?"

"I'll do it tomorrow." Marsh closed his eyes, took a steadying breath. "I'll be up to pick up my wages before Caroline and I go out."

"Your mother didn't get to the bank."

"I can't feed my family on air, Dad."

"We provide accommodation and an employment package."

"I need money too." Marsh heard the distinct snap in his voice. "I work hard and deserve a wage."

Caroline's breath whooshed out—the audible rush of air too soft for most people to hear. Marsh's temper lightened at her obvious surprise since he never argued with his father. His mother either. He grinned at her, amused by her surprise.

"You won't get any wages if that fence doesn't get done today."

Marsh hung up on his blustering father. His marriage wasn't the only thing that needed to change.

Once Marsh left to collect the farm dogs and shift the cattle, Caroline prepared lunch for James and woke him to get ready for school. While he donned his clothes, she woke her three-year-old. He blinked at her, a miniature copy of Marsh with his soft black curls and dancing green eyes.

The thing that had attracted her to Marsh. She'd attended a varsity party with her friend and heard him laughing at a joke. His laugh had made her lips curl and he'd glanced up to catch her staring. Tall, with a broad chest and the look of someone who spent hours outdoors, he wore faded jeans that hugged his muscular thighs and a black T-shirt. Everything about him and his friends screamed sports and popularity, and fascinated, she'd continued to ogle him.

Even now, her cheeks heated at the memory—the intense connection they'd shared across the room. Marsh had broken their gaze, said something to the four friends he'd been standing with, and they'd all turned to stare. She drifted back in years, remembering...

She'd frozen at the interest, her cheeks blazing with color. Mortified, she'd ducked her head and hurried after her girlfriend. When she risked a glance over her shoulder, none of them were laughing but they were still watching her, and she felt even more like prey.

Good grief. She should've stayed at home and finished sewing her dress to wear to the country racing carnival, the one she intended to enter in the Best Dressed competition. Winning the prize would pay part of her university fees and hopefully stretch to textbooks for her design course. But no, she'd allowed her roomie to drag her to the party. Just for a few hours.

She pushed through the throng of dancing, laughing students, murmuring apologies as she jostled people.

"Hey." The touch on her shoulder had her spinning around, the words of apology for pushing dying on her lips.

It was him.

He grinned at her. "My name is Marsh. Who are you?"

12

"Caroline."

His green eyes sparkled as he scanned her face. When an exuberant couple knocked her toward him, he drew her closer until her hand pressed against his chest to maintain her own space. He lifted his head, inhaled, his pectoral muscles rising beneath her fingers. Slowly, he released the breath and beamed at her.

"Would you like to dance or join me and my friends at the bar for a drink?"

"You want to dance with me?" The gorgeous man tangled her tongue. Her eyes, however, worked fine. Taller than her by a good six inches. He had inky-black curls, long enough to skim his collarbone. His green eyes danced with life and laughter, the jade color offset by thick, long eyelashes. He had a strong face, not exactly handsome. His nose was a trifle big for that, but his grin held rakish charm, highlighted by the scruff on his jawline. Her heart beat faster as she stared up at him. "Me?" she repeated, positive she'd misheard.

"Yes." Not a hint of hesitation or teasing.

Caroline nodded. This was a mistake. Men like him didn't pay attention to girls like her. "Do you play rugby?" He had the look of a rugby player as did his friends.

"Yes." Amusement sounded in his voice.

He pulled away and grabbed her hand, twining their fingers together. "We'll go outside on the deck. It's cooler out there and we can still hear the music."

Caroline hesitated.

"There are others dancing out there," Marsh said.

She relaxed once she saw he spoke the truth and allowed him to lead her outside.

"That's better," he said and he dragged in a huge breath, another of those sexy grins shaping his sensual mouth. "I'm a country boy and sometimes the crush of people gets to me. I can breathe out here."

"Where are you from?" she asked, glad of the conversational lead. Shock at his approach had left her mind fuzzy. Off balance. Yeah, definitely off balance.

"Middlemarch. My parents have a farm there. What about you?"

"My parents live in Dunedin. Dad is a plumber and has his own business. My mother is a teacher."

"Are you a student at the university?"

"Yes, I'm studying art and design, specializing in textiles. You?"

He claimed a quiet spot on the deck and pulled her close, his muscular arms cupping her shoulders before one slid behind her back. "Agriculture and business."

His warm breath feathered across her neck, left bared because she'd clipped her hair up in deference to the warm summer night. A shiver worked through her. His scent thrilled her—a hint of citrus aftershave with green and wild undertones. He smelled of the outdoors and clean, healthy male. Much better than the fellow student who'd tried to cop a feel in the lift the other day between classes.

"Do you live at home?"

"No," Caroline said. "My parents wanted me too. Even though it's cheaper, I wanted independence, to make my own decisions, you know? I'm rooming with my best friend in one of the varsity accommodation blocks."

"I'm flatting with friends from Middlemarch," Marsh said. "The guys I was with at the bar. We went to school together and it made sense to share a flat. Brothers? Sisters?"

"I have an older sister. She lives and works in Auckland. She's eight years older than me."

Marsh fell silent and seemed content to sway to the music and hold her. When the music ended, she expected him to thank her and rejoin his friends.

He didn't.

He pulled back so he could see her face. "Would you like to go for coffee? I'd offer to buy you dinner, but a coffee is as far as I can stretch," he said.

"You don't have to buy me a coffee."

"I want to talk to you."

She studied his expression, instantly suspicious, but sincerity blazed from his sexy face. "There is a McDonald's two streets away. I don't have much cash either, but if we pool our resources, we might manage a hamburger each."

"Thank you." He took her hand again. "I'll tell my friends I'm leaving. Do you need to tell anyone?"

She nodded. "I'll send a text to my friend."

Ten minutes later, they entered the fast-food restaurant. With a coffee and a burger each, they'd talked for two hours, learning about each other. Her initial wariness seeped away, leaving the seeds of something else. Friendship. Attraction.

"I have to go," Marsh said.

Caroline glanced at her wristwatch and nodded. "I should leave too. I need to finish making a dress to wear to the races so I have an entry for the Best Dressed contest." She stood, the easy conversation of earlier sticking in her throat. Was this it?

"I had fun," Marsh said. "Can I walk you home?"

Her breath eased out. "Thanks, but it's not necessary. The student accommodation is three blocks."

Marsh reached for her hand and laced their fingers together. "I'll walk you home."

The start of their romance. Marsh had kissed her cheek and left her at her door, appearing at the races the next day, cheering when she'd claimed the runner-up prize in the Best Dressed contest.

"Mum. Mum!" James tugged on her cardigan sleeve, jerking her from the past, their courtship, the good years.

"Yes." She glanced at the clock on the far wall and reached for James's lunch box. "Is your school bag packed? It's time for us to walk you to the bus stop."

After pulling on jackets, Caroline hustled her two boys out the door. They waited at the bus shelter, the bright red school bus puttering along the road four minutes later. With James aboard, she and Ricky wandered back to the house. Once the kitchen was clean again, Caroline turned her mind to packing and remembered she'd lent Marsh's parents their suitcases when they'd gone to Fiji for a holiday.

Great. Just great.

She steeled herself to visit Dawn Rutherford. The woman had never liked her and made no secret of her attitude. She did, however, dote on Ricky, which was why Caroline decided to take her son with her. Hopefully, Ricky's presence would halt Dawn's questions.

A ten-minute car ride later, Caroline pulled up outside Charles and Dawn Rutherford's home. A two-story brick-and-tile home, set like a jewel amongst a lush garden. Dawn had a way with plants and often hosted gardening groups to tour her extensive gardens. Each season, she chose a color theme and even with autumn's arrival the bright beds of red and white roses, petunias and pansies blazed in synchronized perfection.

Caroline dragged in a deep breath to brace herself and turned to Ricky with a bright smile. "Are you ready to visit Grandma?"

Even though Dawn and Charles remained distant to her, they spent time with their grandchildren. In the early days of their marriage, she'd mentioned it to Marsh. He'd shrugged and said they'd always been that way, but he admitted their attitudes had shifted for the worse after his older brother Angus had died in a car crash.

The front door to the house opened and her slim mother-in-law stood waiting. Her gaze flickered over Caroline,

SHELLEY MUNRO

from head to shoes, the scrutiny taking mere seconds but leaving Caroline feeling lacking.

Dawn Rutherford smiled, the light of laughter and humor sloughing away her disapproval. "Who are you?" Her voice bubbled with teasing, love shining in her jade-green eyes. "Do I know you? Have you come to rob my cookie jar?"

"Grandma! Grandma! I'm here!" Ricky shouted gleefully, used to this game. "It's me. Ricky."

Even at this time of the morning, Dawn looked ready to hit the shops or go for coffee. Caroline became acutely conscious of the too-tight shirt that hung over her faded jeans to hide the fact she could no longer fasten the button of the fly. No danger of her trousers sliding to a puddle at her feet.

Caroline followed her excited son up the path, her comfortable runners dragging against the decorative cobblestones. Trepidation tightened her throat and dried her mouth and she resisted the urge to wipe her sweaty palms against her thighs.

"You just caught me," Dawn said in the crisp, no-nonsense voice she reserved for Caroline and sometimes her son. "The girls and I are hitting the shops in Dunedin."

"I won't keep you then," Caroline said, forcing the words across her desert-dry tongue. "I've come to collect the two suitcases we lent you for your trip to Fiji."

"Oh?" Two well-plucked brows rose in punctuation of the unuttered question.

Caroline didn't answer, merely waited. Less is more. *Less is more*.

Dawn huffed out an irritated sigh, her gaze speaking volumes. "I have time for a quick cup of tea, and you can tell me about your upcoming trip. Marsh didn't mention a holiday when he dropped by to speak with Charles. Would you like a hot chocolate and a cookie?"

Ricky nodded with enthusiasm. "Yes, please."

Pride rose in Caroline. He was a good boy. She and Marsh had made awesome children, even if nothing else they did together worked any longer.

Dawn led Ricky inside and Caroline followed. Her mother-in-law had a knack with decorating and colors. The interior of the house formalized the welcome stated by the gardens and façade. Magazine-ready and on the official side. Wooden floorboards gleamed underfoot and an Oriental runner ran the length of the passage from the hall. Caroline dawdled, a trace of envy filling her at the smart cream walls and the framed photographs of Mount Cook and other Otago landmarks even though entering this house made her worry about breakages and clumsiness.

Closer to the kitchen a cluster of framed paintings, bright and bold children's artwork, should have jarred, but they added to the charm. She paused, a quick smile of pride relaxing the stiffness from her shoulders. James had inherited her artistic talent.

"You're dawdling."

With a sigh, Caroline entered the kitchen.

"Sit. Sit," Dawn said.

Caroline rounded the kitchen table and pulled out a chair while watching Ricky and Dawn. Both had jet-black hair and green eyes. Both were slender. Both moved with an animal grace.

A frown pulled at her. God, she had to stop this self-pity. Some marriages didn't work, no matter how hard the parties tried. She needed to grab for bravado and move on. That was what she'd decided, wasn't it?

Dawn bustled around the modern kitchen, chattering to Ricky the entire time and giving him small tasks to help. Soon the peaty scent of one of the exotic teas her mother-in-law favored filled the kitchen. Dawn set two mugs on her black granite counter plus a plate of cookies. She settled Ricky at the small table she kept for the children.

A few minutes later, she poured tea into the china mugs. She handed one to Caroline plus the plate of cookies. Her gaze did that brief scan of Caroline's voluptuous body again, a silent message that Caroline should stay far away from cookies.

"I'll get the milk."

"Thanks." Caroline stared at her mother-in-law's back for an instant then reached for a cookie. She bit into the crisp treat and closed her eyes to savor the chocolate hit. When she opened her eyes, she found Dawn frowning at her.

"Here is the milk."

"Thanks." Caroline tipped a generous portion into her mug to help disguise the strong flavor. She preferred coffee.

Dawn slid into a chair and cupped her mug in her hands. "Why do you need the suitcases?"

Caroline considered lying, then straightened her shoulders. She looked her mother-in-law in the eye. "Marsh and I are separating. I am moving back to Dunedin."

Dawn had an impassive face unless she wanted to broadcast her emotions. Caroline caught surprise then a trace of satisfaction before the woman's features blanked. She was pleased—happy—she and Marsh were splitting up. "Oh, I'm sorry to hear that."

Caroline didn't believe her for a minute. "So, the suitcases?"

"I'll get them for you. They're in the spare bedroom."

"Thank you." Caroline took a sip of the hated tea to rinse the dryness from her mouth. Her stomach swooped and writhed and her entire body prickled with perspiration, but she slouched with relief. That hadn't been as difficult as she thought.

"I suppose we can babysit while Marsh is working. It shouldn't be too difficult. James and Ricky are good boys."

Alarm, followed by determination, bolted Caroline from her slump. Her spine hit the chair. "There won't be any need for babysitters. James and Ricky are going to Dunedin with me."

"No."

Caroline jumped to her feet, the chair scraping across the tiled floor of the kitchen with a nail-on-blackboard shriek. "We are leaving this afternoon. I want to get the boys settled and—"

21

Dawn stood too, temper and determination in the set of her jaw. "No, I won't allow it."

Fury swept Caroline, and for once, she stood her ground and spoke her mind. "James and Ricky are my sons. They will stay with me. This is not your business and you need to butt out of our marriage. I'll take my suitcases now. Ricky, we're going home."

Chapter 2

Cease This Nonsense

D awn Rutherford stared after the departing vehicle. Those boys couldn't leave Middlemarch. Her grandsons bore feline genes. They'd shift to feline in their teens. City living and felines were a bad combination.

Marsh's fault for marrying a human.

An unplanned pregnancy didn't mean he had to marry the girl.

Stubborn lad. He'd always acted contrary, insisting on going to university and earning the money to go by shearing sheep during every holiday. If he'd stayed on the farm to help Charles, this wouldn't be an issue. If he'd married one of the local girls as they'd wanted him to, but no, Marsh had gone his own way, which had been the polar opposite to their wishes.

Things would have been different if Angus hadn't died. He'd been the eldest, a good son, a dutiful son.

Tears pricked her eyes as she thought of her beloved son, cut down in a senseless car accident. Killed by a human and...no. That was enough of the past. She needed to focus on the future. Dawn trudged inside, the pain still as fresh as when it had happened.

She glanced at her watch and sighed. The shopping excursion didn't hold the same appeal it had earlier. About to cancel, the crunch of car tires on the gravel parking area outside indicated Anita's arrival. She hurried to the bedroom and scooped her handbag off the queen-size bed. Her friend might have a solution. Those boys needed to stay in Middlemarch.

Anita pounded on the front door. A widow in her mid-thirties, she was younger than Dawn but the two women got on well. The door opened before Dawn reached it and Anita stood there beaming.

"I've got my comfortable shoes, and I'm ready to hit the shops." Anita wore her black hair pulled back in a braid, had highlighted her pink lips with a berry-colored lipstick while her sparkling green eyes appeared more dramatic with judicious use of eyeliner and mascara. She was a stunning beauty but spoke little of her marriage. Her husband had been much older and his adult children had created friction within the relationship. That was all Dawn knew. While Anita had an active social life, she didn't intend to tie herself to a man again.

"I think I'll stay at home after all." She pulled a face. "My shopping mood has vacated the building."

Anita grasped her forearm and tugged. "You have your handbag. We're going. If you've had a crappy morning, you can unload during the drive to Dunedin. No, don't argue."

"All right." Discussing it with Anita might help. She'd make a better listener than Charles. Her husband tended to bluster and shout, which achieved nothing. "Let me get my shoes, and I'll be ready."

"Good." Anita grinned. "How does a foot massage and a pedicure sound to you? I have a voucher for a new spa place that has just opened, and I've made appointments for this afternoon. We'll recover from our morning shopping with lunch and spa pampering. We're meeting the others at the mall."

Five minutes later, Anita sped along the road, heading for Dunedin.

"Tell me what has you so silent and brooding," Anita said.

Dawn told her everything.

"Oh dear. That is a pickle."

Dawn snorted out a laugh, feeling better for sharing the problem. "What should we do?"

"Have you spoken to Marsh?"

"Not yet, but he's made it clear in the past he won't listen to our advice." Dawn pressed a hand against her breastbone in an attempt to alleviate the stress of the situation. Easy to see her past mistakes now. "I—we—didn't approve of the marriage and made our stance obvious. If we'd—"

"No point worrying about maybes or regrets," Anita cut in as she overtook a tractor. "You need to take action now. Have you considered approaching the Feline council with the problem? They're always saying they're there for the community, and this can't be the first time this has happened. Perhaps they'll have a solution—something you haven't considered."

Dawn considered that and nodded. "I'll ring Valerie now."

She dialed the feline elder and spoke rapidly, outlining the problem.

"We have a meeting in an hour," Valerie said. "I'll get back to you."

Marsh arrived home from shifting the stock to find Caroline packing. "What's going on? I thought we were going for coffee." He eyed the bags on top of the bed, the neat piles of clothes.

"Marsh, I can't go on like this. Our marriage isn't working, and I c-can't take it any longer."

Fear ripped through him, clamping around his ribs so hard he had to fight to breathe. Caroline couldn't leave him. Surely there was something they could do, a compromise. Resolve forced him to speak. "Let's get that coffee. You can tell me what you want to do."

"We don't have to go for coffee."

"Ricky can play and we can sit outside and talk. It's neutral ground and the public place will keep us both calm." At least he hoped he could control his feline.

"I...all right," she said finally.

A small victory. He balled his fingers and sharp nails sliced his palm. Damn feline was close to the surface. He sucked in a deep breath, struggling for calm.

"I'd better change."

"Why? You look fine as you are." She'd pulled her strawberry-blonde hair back in a ponytail and wisps had escaped to frame her face. The pale pink T-shirt she'd changed into after a quick shower hugged her curves while faded jeans completed her outfit.

"I should go on a diet." She lifted her chin, pained blue eyes challenging him.

"I think you look gorgeous," he said without hesitation and reached for her hand. His feline found comfort in the physical contact and a soft purr played through Marsh's mind.

"Let me change my jeans."

"I'll organize Ricky while you do that," Marsh said.

She nodded and scuttled from the room like a spooked sheep.

Marsh exhaled, knowing he had a difficult task ahead. Their marriage had drifted for months, the last year. Somehow, he had to fix this mess because, if there was one fact he knew, it was he wanted Caroline as his wife.

Ricky was playing in his bedroom, the *broom-broom* noises making Marsh smile. Marsh stopped at the doorway, opened his mouth to speak and paused.

"What are you doing, son?"

Ricky turned, a guilty expression on his face. "Painting."

"I don't think Mum will approve of you painting on the wall." Caroline walked up behind and craned to peer over his shoulder. Instead of moving, he stayed put so she'd have to squeeze next to him.

"Are those James's paints?"

"Ricky?" Marsh prompted.

"Yes," Ricky whispered, his gaze skittering away.

"James didn't say you could borrow his paints," Caroline said.

"No," Ricky whispered again, still not looking at either of them.

Marsh tried not to laugh because not only had Ricky painted what he thought was roads on the wall with a square-looking truck, but he'd spilled a fair amount of paint on his clothes.

"Lucky for us your mother got water colors," Caroline muttered.

"I'll get something to clean off the wall," Marsh said. "You deal with Ricky."

It was over an hour later when they set off for Storm in a Teacup since Ricky had managed to get paint over his duvet cover as well.

A coach load of people exited the café as they entered. Every table bore dirty dishes and people waited at the counter for service. Emily Mitchell, the owner, looked up with a smile.

"On your own?" Marsh asked.

"Yes."

"Why don't you grab us a table outside and settle Ricky? I'll clear the tables for Emily and order our coffee," Marsh said. "A latte for you?"

"With trim milk please." Caroline led their son around to the garden entrance.

Marsh heard a gleeful shout from Ricky and an answering one from another child. Good. Someone to play with would keep their son occupied while they talked.

Marsh cleared tables and rounded the counter to stack them in the kitchen. The place looked like a bombsite. Caroline arrived a few minutes later with a tray of plates and cups from outside.

"Ricky is playing with Susan Longford's boy. Susan said she'd watch them," Caroline said. "I'll stack the dishwasher."

They worked as a team, helping Emily Mitchell with the backload of dishes and stocking up her food cabinet. Marsh found himself wishing their marriage worked as smoothly. Tomasine Mitchell and Isabella Mitchell, Emily's sisters-in-law, arrived and took over. They'd been working for almost two hours.

"Thank you so much," Emily said, beaming at them. Her brown eyes held sincere thanks, her cheeks flushed from rushing. "My helper called in sick and I've had two coach loads this morning, neither of whom booked. I presume you came in for coffee. What can I get you?"

"Two lattes with trim milk please," Marsh said.

"Anything to eat?"

Marsh thought of his empty wallet with frustration, a hint of anger. "No, thanks."

The bell over the café door tinkled. Marsh had always thought the sound welcoming, just like the owner. His nostrils flared as he identified another feline male, and he shifted his body position, moving closer to Caroline in a patent statement of ownership.

"Saber," Emily said with delight. "You're too late to help with the rush. Marsh and Caroline probably wish they hadn't come for coffee when they did because they've spent the last two hours helping me."

"Kitten," Saber replied and gave his mate a quick kiss.

Marsh nodded at the oldest of the Mitchell brothers. He'd gone to school with Leo, the middle brother, so he didn't know Saber well, although he'd know he was a Mitchell at first glance since the brothers were similar in appearance. Feline-green eyes, black hair and brutal on the rugby field.

"Marsh. Caroline." Saber nodded a greeting.

"Grab a seat." Emily made a scooting motion with her hands. "I'll bring your coffee." She headed for the kitchen, pausing to speak to Tomasine, the petite shifter manning the espresso machine, and disappeared out the back. Saber ambled after his mate.

"I hope Ricky has been behaving," Caroline said into the resulting silence.

"We haven't heard war-whoops. That's a good sign." Marsh placed a hand on the small of her back to guide her outside, and a part of him died when she stiffened at his touch. She couldn't leave him, not after he'd gone against his parents to marry her. If only he'd... He shoved aside the self-doubt and steeled his resolution.

He'd made mistakes, but it wasn't too late.

He refused to let her walk without a fight.

He needed to show her by action and deed.

They claimed a table in partial shade, Caroline gravitating to the seat screened from direct sunshine. It was hot for this time of the year, but signs of the approaching winter showed in the gold, yellow and red colors of the leaves.

Marsh glanced at Caroline, the firm set of her jaw and cursed the circumstances. "Please don't go, Caroline. I love you and the boys."

She swallowed, a beam of sunlight striking her hair and highlighting the red tones. "I can't go on this way. We don't talk. We don't share a room. We don't have a marriage."

Pain pierced his chest at the truths she spoke. And they were the surface of the problem. They struggled to pay the bills because his father didn't pay him half the time. In hindsight he could see he'd fucked this up and there was no one else to blame.

31

E mily Mitchell stared at her mate as he prowled around the café kitchen for a second time. As he stalked past, ready for a third circuit, she wrenched on his arm and yanked him to a stop. "What is it? What's wrong?"

Saber grimaced and ran a hand through his hair. "The council meeting."

Amusement bubbled to the fore. "You could always retire."

"Want to. Can't. Promised Uncle Herbert I'd keep them in line. He threatened to haunt me if I didn't take his seat on the council."

"That sounds like a threat."

Saber scowled and scratched his head, disordering his hair yet again. "It was a promise, which is why I can't go back on my word. God, I loved that old man. He held us together after our parents died, kept us in a family unit when others thought we were too much trouble."

"You've never told me this before. I mean, I know about your uncle, but not that the authorities considered splitting up you and your brothers."

"It was the council. We felines try to keep any problems involving our community in-house. Uncle Herbert told the council he was keeping us, and there would be no argument about his decision. They wanted to split us up and place us with other families who didn't have children. Thank god, Uncle Herbert got his way. He helped us heal."

"He did an excellent job."

"Yeah." Saber started to pace again.

"Saber, for goodness' sake. What happened at the council meeting?"

"Marsh and Caroline Rutherford."

Emily pulled a large china bowl from the shelf and set it on the counter. "What about Marsh and Caroline? Are they in trouble? I don't know either of them well, just to say hello. They don't come to the café very often."

"According to Valerie, they're separating. Caroline is leaving Marsh and taking the boys to Dunedin. They want me to talk to them." He grimaced.

"Interfere in a marriage. That doesn't sound like a good idea."

"That's what I said. They voted and I was it before I knew what hit me." Saber huffed out a breath, distracting her with the flexing of his chest.

A very magnificent chest. When he started his prowling again, she reached out to pinch his bum. He jumped, and she laughed aloud at his disgruntled expression.

"I need help."

She crossed the room to join him and stood on tiptoe to press a kiss on his lips. "You could ignore the council." When his arms came around her, she cuddled closer.

"Ignoring the problem won't work. They're tenacious."

"I like Marsh and Caroline, even though I don't know them well. They pitched in to help me today without a word. Not many people would do that." A thought formed and she pulled back a fraction. "I might have an idea."

"Tell me. Anything. If you have a plan that will work, I'll take time off, and we'll go on the honeymoon we've talked about for the last year. And you'll get lucky tonight. That's a promise."

Emily grinned. "High stakes, although I'm lucky all the time."

"I love you. I like to make you happy."

She caressed his cheek. "You do make me happy. I'd like to go to Rotorua and Taupo. One week at each place."

"Two weeks?"

"Two weeks," she confirmed.

"All right. It's a deal. What have you got?"

She reached up to tap his nose. "Not so fast. There is something else."

His eyes narrowed. "What?"

"Just to show I play fair, I'll give you my idea first. Invite Caroline and Marsh to join us tonight for dinner. Your brothers are already coming for a barbeque. Two more adults and their two sons won't make any difference. Sylvie would love to have kids to play with."

"Not a bad idea. That will give me a chance to see how they are together," Saber mused. "And if I get the right vibe, I could take Marsh aside and have a word with him."

"If it helps, they both look at each other when they think the other isn't looking," Emily said.

"Do they now? Interesting." Saber nodded, apparently coming to a decision. "One thing, kitten. Caroline doesn't know about feline shifters. She doesn't know about Marsh or that her two boys are felines."

"Oh. That makes things tricky for Marsh."

"Yes." Saber's voice held disapproval. "His parents doing."

"Emily," Tomasine called. "Your coffee is ready."

"Be there in a sec," Emily answered. "We should invite ourselves to join Marsh and Caroline for coffee. Ask them to dinner while we're sitting with them."

"Sometimes your sneakiness scares me," Saber said. "Let's do this. Wait, what was the other thing you wanted in exchange for your idea?"

"The getting lucky." Emily winked at him. "It's time for me to visit Gavin and have another birth control shot. I was thinking I'd go off birth control, and we should start practicing for real."

"A baby?"

"Emily!" Tomasine called.

"Coming." Emily hurried past her mate, rather enjoying his nonplussed expression. She felt his gaze on her back and put an extra sway in her walk. Yep, their upcoming holiday would be full of hot loving, like a real honeymoon. She couldn't wait.

"D o you mind if we join you?" Emily asked.

Caroline smiled, and Marsh saw the relief in her because she wouldn't have to spend time alone with him. "We'd enjoy the company."

She'd doodled on a bit of paper, drawing Ricky and his friend playing, instead of concentrating on their problems. Frustration had his feline struggling to surface, and he dragged in a deep breath, scrambling for control. He sensed Saber's quick glance, but didn't meet his gaze.

"I brought blueberry muffins," Emily said.

"Thanks, but no." A flash of heat rose to the surface in Caroline's cheeks.

"I only have enough money for coffee." Stiff pride filled Marsh's words.

"Are you kidding?" Emily grinned at him, wrinkling her nose. "Your money is no good here today. You both worked your butts off to help me. The least I can do is give you coffee and muffins in exchange. I've brought a gingerbread man and a fluffy for your son. Sorry, my mind has gone blank on his name."

"Ricky," Caroline said.

"Thank you." Marsh stood. "I'll grab him." He wandered over to Susan. Ricky and her son were playing with trucks and tractors in the sandpit. Susan looked up from her book at his approach. "Thanks for looking after Ricky."

"Are you kidding? Ricky has kept my son entertained, and I've read my book in peace. A luxury!"

"Ricky, we have a fluffy for you."

Ricky made one last *broom-broom* noise as he crashed his tractor into a grader. When both vehicles flipped with the force of the crash, he let out a cheer and sprang to his feet. "Bye." He waved and sprinted off to join Caroline and the Mitchells.

"Ricky says thank you," Marsh said dryly.

Susan waved him off with a laugh and started packing up toys and her book. "No prob. We should be going anyway."

Marsh wandered back to join Caroline and slid into his seat.

"I didn't realize your wife was so talented," Emily said.

"She is," Marsh agreed and meant every word. Caroline had a way with art and handicrafts. "James has the same artistic talent. Ricky takes after me."

"We're having a barbecue tonight," Emily said. "It will be us, Felix and Leo and their wives. We'd love you to join us."

Caroline glanced at him. "Thanks, but I think—"

Emily reached out and placed her hand over Caroline's. "Please, you'd be doing me a favor. Sylvie would love to have someone to play with instead of it being just adults."

"I...ah..."

Marsh held his breath as Emily squeezed Caroline's hand in silent entreaty. Caroline sucked in her breath, and he could see the tick of her thoughts, the frustrated confusion. Finally, she nodded, forced a smile.

"Thank you. That sounds lovely." Her voice cracked, and guilt sped through Marsh. He'd done this, put this stressed expression on her face. No more regrets or apologies. Instead, he'd come up with a plan and act on it because he loved his boys. He loved Caroline, and if she left, his heart would leave with her.

Marsh swallowed and glanced up to find Saber scrutinizing him. The older feline showed none of his thoughts on his face, but something he saw or decided relaxed his expression into open friendliness.

"Word is stock has vanished from two of the farms bordering our land," Saber said. "Have you lost any stock to rustlers?"

"First, I've heard of it." Marsh shrugged. "I don't get out much." Lack of money and long work hours did that to a man.

Saber sipped his coffee. "Alex Baxter has lost fifty head of his prime stud stock. They were there when he retired for the night and gone when he woke in the morning."

"What did the cops say?"

Saber snorted. "Our local cops have the sense of a gnat. They say they're doing extra patrols and investigating, but you can't do much if you drink coffee and sit at your desk all day."

"Isn't Hannah, the head cop, about to retire? I think Dad mentioned that."

"Yeah, and he doesn't want to break a fingernail before his time is up. Those bodies that turned up have scared the shit out of him. He seems afraid of his own shadow."

Marsh glanced at Caroline and leaned closer to Saber. "Can't the council do something?"

"We've discussed it." Saber's eyes narrowed a fraction and cast a speculative look at Caroline before turning his attention back to Marsh. "We'll hold a meeting of the feline farmers and organize a night patrol."

Marsh nodded, accepting his father would volunteer him for patrol. More excuses to make up for Caroline although he could mention the cattle thieves. A yawn escaped him and he slapped his hand over his mouth. "Sorry. I've been working long hours."

"I thought your father employed two farmhands."

"One left."

"It's hard to get good farm labor."

Marsh's breath rushed out in a frustrated sigh. "Dad isn't the easiest boss. They get sick of him expecting them to work seven days with no time off. It wouldn't surprise me if Jason upped and left too."

Saber drained the last of his coffee and set his cup on the wooden table. "Guess I'd better get going. Felix and Leo will be waiting for me. We're going to sell some cattle before winter sets in and have to decide which ones will go to the sale. I'll see you both tonight."

"What time should we arrive?" Caroline asked. "And should we bring anything? I could make bread if you like?"

"Fresh bread?" At Caroline's nod, Emily beamed. "Yes please. That sounds lovely." She stood. "I'd better get back to work or my assistants will go on strike. Thanks for the help today."

Saber and Emily disappeared into the café, but not before Marsh noticed Saber's hand slide over Emily's butt. He grinned and met Caroline's gaze. Her blue eyes swam with sadness before Ricky grabbed her attention.

Marsh's phone chimed, and he glanced at the screen. His father. He ignored the call and slipped the phone into his pocket.

"I'm out of flour. Do we have enough money to buy flour and pumpkin seeds?"

"Will twelve dollars cover it?"

Caroline nodded.

Marsh stood. "Let's hit the store then."

After a quick stop at the store, Marsh drove them home.

"Emily is good company," Caroline said. "I've never really chatted with her—nothing more than a hello. I know Tomasine better because I see her if I drop off or pick up James from school."

"Leo was in my class at school, but I've lost touch since our marriage." Whenever he shifted, he ran with his parents or the immediate neighbors. His father attended the district feline meetings and passed on the relevant information to him. He hadn't realized how isolated he'd become after working long hours on the farm. His father attended the sales, purchased and sold stock and took care of picking up supplies, which meant Marsh went days without seeing other people—human or feline. Part of the reason he wanted to play rugby again. "I'm looking forward to seeing him again. You'll like Leo."

"His wife Isabella seems nice," Caroline said. "Sometimes she drops off Sylvie for Tomasine."

"I can pick up James from school this afternoon."

"Won't you be busy on the farm?"

"No. I told Dad I was taking the rest of the day off. Ricky can come with me if you want."

"I'm hoping Ricky will have a sleep this afternoon since we're going out tonight," Caroline said. "But if he's awake, he'd enjoy going out with you."

Another salvo of guilt struck Marsh mid-chest, and it reverberated through his body, poking and prodding at his insecurities. Crap. He'd been an absent husband and father. Another item for his list.

"Can I help with the bread?"

Caroline sent him a startled look. "You want to help?"

"If I can."

"How about if you and Ricky pick herbs for me and cut some silver beet? I'll make focaccia bread."

Marsh pulled into their driveway to find his father on the doorstep. "We can do that. Let me see what Dad wants then I'm all yours." Marsh caught the faint tightening of her facial muscles, the flash of doubt and it steeled his determination. "Five minutes," he promised.

Caroline unbuckled Ricky from his car seat and led him inside, leaving Marsh alone with his father.

"Dawn said Caroline is leaving you."

Marsh didn't reply.

His father muttered an oath. "You can't let her take the boys. They won't survive in the city. They'll need you once they reach their teen years."

41

Marsh reined in his temper, reached for calm. "My marriage is none of your business, Dad. I need you and Mum to butt out."

"I knew this would turn into a bloody mess. No good comes of a human-feline pairing."

"Why were you ringing me?"

"Jason has handed in his notice. I need you to drive to the top ridge and round up the cattle. Don't like the look of the weather. I'd prefer it if they were in the winter pastures. If you leave now, you should be finished by the day after tomorrow."

Marsh stared at his father in disbelief. "I thought you expected me to keep my sons."

Charles flapped his right hand in impatience. "I'll take care of that for you. Dawn and I will come and collect your boys and keep them with us."

Marsh felt his mouth drop open. He snapped it shut hard enough for his teeth to clack. "What about Caroline?"

"What's she gonna do?" Charles snorted. "Call the cops?"

"Caroline, the boys and I are going out for dinner tonight."

"You need to get moving on the stock roundup."

"No."

Charles's brows shot upward. "I'm not too old to take you down, boy. Angus would never—"

"I'm not my brother. Angus is dead, Dad. I'm taking the rest of the day off. If you want the cattle rounded up, I suggest you start. I'll drive up tomorrow." Before his father could speak, Marsh walked away, hands bunched to fists at his sides.

His father's curse and fury rumbled after him. "I can sack you."

Marsh ignored the threat and strode to the front door of the farmhouse. He ripped open the door and marched inside, shutting his father out with a firm click.

A hollow victory, but one long coming. About time his parents accepted Angus's death was a tragic accident. He'd survived the crash, but that didn't make him the villain.

Chapter 3

Step Out Of Routine

"We haven't been to a party before," James said.

Marsh exchanged a glance with Caroline, and she looked away first. No, they didn't go out often, and normally, she'd look upon this as a treat. Not this time. Not with apprehension and uncertainty filling her belly. Not with her mind full of things to do once she and the boys reached Dunedin.

"Ricky and I had fun helping to make the bread for the party," Marsh said as they turned onto the road where the Mitchells lived. "I can't wait to eat my share."

"We played soccer with the other boys," James said. "Can we do that again, Daddy?"

Surprise had her looking at Marsh again. He turned into a driveway and pulled up outside a sprawling stone house, surrounded by gardens full of colorful flowers. Warm and welcoming, some of the tension in her gut released.

"We'll play again," Marsh promised, his gaze on her.

God, she wanted to believe Marsh would change, that their life could change. Deep down, though, doubts whooped and hollered, warning explosions going off like fireworks at a Guy Fawkes extravaganza.

They weren't living.

They were existing from day to day, and none of them were doing well with the humdrum subsistence.

The front door of the house sprang open, and Emily and Saber stood there with welcoming smiles on their faces.

"You made it," Emily said, as if she thought they might have changed their minds.

Marsh unbuckled the kids from their car seats while she retrieved the bread.

Saber shook Marsh's hand. "I'm glad you came. Leo said he hasn't seen you for months."

"No, the farm work keeps me busy."

"The bread smells good," Emily said. "Come inside. I left Felix and Leo in charge of the grill. They're still in training, so I daren't leave them alone for long."

Saber chuckled, and Caroline found herself smiling too. It was obvious this couple, this family, was close. It made her wish things were different.

Emily ushered them through the house—a mixture of old and new. A home. Emily carted the bread into the kitchen and rejoined them, guiding them to the dining room. Caroline caught a whiff of lemon furniture polish, the mouth-watering combo of garlic and butter, and when they walked through the double doors of the dining room and outside again, the aroma of grilling meat teased her.

"Smells good," Marsh said and greeted the Mitchell brothers.

"Caroline," Leo said, offering his hand. "I'm glad Emily talked you into coming tonight."

Leo Mitchell had the face of a beautiful angel. Although he resembled his older brothers, his face was symmetrical and his broad welcoming smile took his visage to gorgeous. Bemused, she shook his hand before greeting Felix who she knew better. His features were rougher, more aggressively masculine.

"Saber, I'm putting you in charge while I organize the rest of our dinner. Don't let your brothers burn the steaks," Emily ordered.

"Can I help?" Caroline asked.

The children were playing together in a frantic game of chase, their childish shrieks bringing a smile to her lips.

"Not much to do, except arrange the food on the table," Emily said. "You're welcome to help carry bowls. Where did you buy your dress? I haven't seen anything like it in the stores. The color is gorgeous on you."

Caroline followed Emily back into the house. "Thanks. I made it last year."

"Wow. I've always wanted to learn to sew. Knitting is my limit, when time permits."

"I enjoy knitting too," Caroline said. "I make the boys clothes."

"Tomasine. Isabella. Do you both know Caroline?" Emily asked when they reached the kitchen.

"We run into each other while doing the school run," Isabella said and smiled. "Nice dress. I need new clothes. Where did you buy it? In Dunedin?"

"She made it herself," Emily answered before Caroline could utter a word.

Tomasine walked around Caroline and said, "I want one. Would you make me a dress? I'll pay you. Could we do a girl's trip to Dunedin to buy fabric and patterns?"

"I don't need a pattern," Caroline said. "If you tell me what you want, I can draft a pattern."

"I can't sew to save myself." Tomasine's eyes rounded. "Let's talk later."

Emily pointed to the food sitting on the counter. "These bowls need to go outside plus the cutlery and the plates."

Caroline picked up a bowl of lettuce salad and one of potato salad and followed Emily.

"Meat is ready," Saber called.

Emily set a macaroni salad and sliced tomatoes and cucumber on a sturdy wooden picnic table. "The platter is in the kitchen."

"I'll get it," Felix said.

Isabella came out with the focaccia bread and a stack of knives and forks. Tomasine followed with plates. Felix trotted out with the platter, transferred the meat from the grill and placed it with the rest of the food.

"Dinner is ready," Emily called.

Caroline organized meals for the boys and turned to grab something for herself. Marsh handed her a plate, and it was the food she would've chosen if she'd done it herself. "Thanks."

"You're welcome." He patted the seat beside him. "I've saved you a spot."

Caroline hesitated and found herself the center of attention. A swift kick of heat surged to her cheeks as she slid onto the long bench seat beside Marsh.

"Caroline offered to design and sew dresses for us," Tomasine told her husband. "She made her dress. It's an original."

Isabella laughed. "We bullied her into offering."

"Have you told Caroline about the new weekend market?" Saber asked.

"No! My first thoughts were purely selfish," Emily said with a chuckle.

"Same with me and Tom," Isabella agreed. "It's hard to buy nice clothes when we're stuck in Middlemarch." She winged a wink toward her husband, offered him a cheeky grin.

Caroline's cheeks heated as the entire Mitchell family turned to her. She'd resemble a story-book clown since a blush clashed with her hair and glowed against her fair skin.

"Caroline makes the boys' clothes, and she made my shirt," Marsh said.

Caroline stilled, her chest squeezing so tight she had to gasp for her next breath of air. He sounded proud of her, almost as pleased as if they'd complimented him. She hadn't even realized he'd known she made the boys' clothes. His mother always turned up her nose...she'd given the trousers Marsh wore to him for his birthday.

Emily picked up a piece of focaccia and took a bite. She swallowed. "The bread is delicious, so you can cook as well. Good to know for when I need help in the café. I'm teaching Tomasine and Isabella how to cook everything on our menu, but neither of them enjoy baking as much as I do."

"I don't get much spare time," Caroline said with real regret. She'd love to earn extra money but between her obligations to the after-school group and her duties on the farm—feeding the chickens and cooking for the shearers and doing the other odd-jobs Dawn foisted on her, fitting in another job might be difficult.

Marsh shot her a surprised look, and Caroline squirmed. "Your mother wants me to help her with the cooking when the shearing gang arrives."

"But she—" He broke off, the line between his brows becoming more prominent. "I see."

After an uncomfortable silence, Emily nudged the conversation into a discussion of the upcoming zombie run.

"We're leaving it late in the season," Felix said. "I hope it doesn't snow."

"If it does, we might need to change the obstacles," Leo said.

"I think it will be okay since there will be spotters on the course. It's only five kilometers and the competitors can use the new shower block and changing rooms at the sports ground," Saber said. "Emily is organizing a hot punch for competitors."

"Sam and Lisa said they were coming. They asked me to be on their team," Emily said.

"You?" Felix asked.

Caroline caught the humorous glint in Saber's eyes as he studied his wife.

"Yes me." Emily lifted her nose. "I thought it might be fun, and Sam and Lisa have confidence in me. They're bringing Henry and Gerard. It sounds as if they've decided to start their security business in Middlemarch. I liked them both."

"Sam, your cousin?" Marsh asked.

"Yeah. He mat—married Lisa Jordan. They live not far from Christchurch. Sam breeds and trains horses and he has cattle. A few sheep from memory," Saber said.

"I heard they had another earthquake yesterday," Caroline said. "I think they said it was a 5.7. Are they okay?"

Emily nodded. "I spoke with Lisa. She said they escaped damage although they felt the quake. Anyway, the race will be a challenge. Maybe Isabella or Tomasine can man the hot drinks."

"Sorry," Isabella said. "Tom and I are running. We're looking for two more women to round out our team."

"Could Caroline and I do the drinks?" Marsh glanced at her. "We could do that, couldn't we?"

"No," she said. "Remember, I'll be in Dunedin." Her cheeks heated again when everyone stared at her. No, it was her imagination. Not all the Mitchells were looking at her. Just Saber and Emily.

"Never mind," Emily said. "I'm sure I can find someone to replace me."

"I thought you'd enjoy dressing as a zombie," Saber said. "But if you want to race, that's fine. I'll enjoy looking at your legs more than zombie makeup."

The couple grinned at each other, and Caroline saw their open love and affection for each other. Their happiness made her sad, made her envious, made her want to cry. Marsh had used to look at her like that. She glanced at her husband and her breath caught. That wasn't indifference she saw in his eyes.

Seeing the yearning in Caroline was a punch to the chest. A strike that laid open every mistake he'd made in their relationship. In that instant, he knew his parents were wrong. He should've gone with his gut instincts and honesty. Now it was too late.

"I started to tell you about the craft fair that's starting," Emily said and set her cutlery across her empty plate.

"Has everyone eaten enough?" Saber asked. At their nods, he stood and cleared the dirty plates. "Why don't we let the ladies relax and we'll take care of the cleanup."

Marsh had no problem with that. He helped around the home as much as he could, although working long hours meant he missed most meals with Caroline and the boys. He stood and collected several empty plates before following Leo inside the house.

"I wanted to talk to you," Saber said. "Felix and Leo will do the dishes while we speak in my office."

Marsh froze and forced a smile. "Why do I feel as if I've been called to the principal's office?"

"Believe me, if the elders hadn't forced me into this conversation..." A heavy sigh gusted from him, and he gestured for Marsh to follow. "We don't have long to speak before the women wonder where we are."

Saber strode down a passage and opened the first door. He gestured Marsh inside and closed it behind them with a firm click. "Grab a seat."

Marsh dropped onto the wooden chair set in front of the large desk. "Sounds serious." He glanced at the bookcases and the display of livestock awards before turning his attention back to Saber. "What's wrong?"

Saber scowled. "I didn't want to become involved, but the elders insisted. It has come to the Feline council's attention that Caroline intends to leave you and take your children to the city."

"The local grapevine works fast. My mother, I presume." Marsh stared at Saber without blinking, his pulse rate kicking into choppy at issuing the silent challenge. "Most people think a man's marriage is no one else's business except his own."

"I agree," Saber said. "But I want to offer my help, regardless. I can see you love her. I heard Caroline knows nothing of the feline community. Is that right?"

Tension banded Marsh's chest, tightening his muscles until his feline longed for movement. Before the thought fully formed, he sprang to his feet and started to pace. "Yes. It's true."

"Why? Women hate secrets. I know that from experience."

"Don't you think I know that? I've known that for years, but now I've lied to my wife I'm stuck. We've been married for six years. The longer I kept things from Caroline, the harder it was to tell her the truth. That I'm a feline shifter and our sons have inherited to ability to shift."

"You can't let Caroline take them to the city. My niece shifted, and she has just turned six. What happens if they shift in the city?"

"I can't take the boys from Caroline. She's their mother."

"Why didn't you tell her?"

"My parents weren't in favor of the marriage. Caroline got pregnant. I loved her and wanted to get married. My parents wanted a feline daughter-in-law. They tried to get me to change my mind, said the marriage would fail, and I'd be placing the Middlemarch felines in danger if I told Caroline the truth. They went on and on and I gave in for the sake of peace. A mistake. I shouldn't have taken their advice." Marsh huffed out a breath that ended in a cynical laugh. "It was a miscalculation returning to Middlemarch. Dad expects me to work long hours and refuses to pay me—" Marsh dragged his right hand through his hair and resumed pacing.

"Your brother Angus."

Marsh froze and swung to face Saber. "What about Angus?"

"Rumor says your parents were distraught when he died, that they expected him to take over the farm."

"Yes."

"They blame you for the accident?"

"Yes." The reply emerged through his clenched teeth.

"What about getting a job elsewhere?" Saber asked.

"I tried to get a job on another property. Dad refused to give me a reference. In fact, he rang the owners of the cattle station and told them I was inexperienced and untrustworthy, that he had to supervise me since I couldn't think for myself."

Shock showed in Saber's face before he wiped his expression clean. "All right. Answer me this. Do you want to save your marriage?"

"Yes. I love Caroline. There is no else for me. I wanted her from the first moment I saw her, and my mind hasn't changed."

"She isn't marked. She doesn't smell feline, not like Emily."

"When I promised my parents I'd keep the truth from Caroline, it meant I couldn't mark her."

"Caroline isn't your true mate."

Anguish filled Marsh, torment at the mistakes he'd made with his marriage and their lives. "Caroline is my mate."

"Saul's uncle is hiring," Saber said, changing the subject. "You remember Saul Sinclair?"

"Yes, although I haven't seen him for ages."

"Cam Sinclair has a farm in the Mackenzie region. Felix worked there for a few months and now that he's returned to Middlemarch, Cam is looking for a replacement. He wants someone experienced who is willing to learn new things and work with others. His preference is for a married couple since his wife needs help with cooking. Wages are decent, competitive with other stations, and he offers a five-day week and accommodation. The station is remote, so they run a correspondence school for the kids. I think Felix said there were ten children and one of the other wives is a teacher. She runs the schooling side. Are you interested? You have a partial degree and you're a hard worker. I could put a word in for you with Cam."

Marsh sank back onto the chair and stared at Saber, almost too afraid to take his words at face value.

"Do you think Caroline would consider giving your marriage a second chance if you made a new start?"

"A wage and a five-day workweek?"

"I presume you'd need to work longer hours during lambing and other busy times of the year, but, according to Felix, Cam thinks the men work better with regular time off."

"How long do I have to make my decision?"

"Not long. If Cam doesn't hear from me by Friday, he intends to place an ad in the national farming magazine."

"Two days. I'll talk to Caroline tonight. Is it possible for me to talk to Cam Sinclair?"

"I'll give you his number, so you can ring him tomorrow. Take Felix aside and ask your questions. He can tell you about the living situation and the other men."

Marsh nodded, a surge of hope lifting his chin. "I'll do that. Thanks." He extended his hand and Saber clasped it in a firm shake.

Saber stood. "My final word of advice—tell Caroline the truth. Your parents were wrong to insist on you keeping this secret. If Caroline is your mate, she deserves the truth."

Caroline sat in the passenger seat of the old Toyota and wished she'd met Emily, Tomasine and Isabella earlier, rather than staying in the nodding-acquaintance zone. They'd been nice to her, treated her as worthy rather than an encumbrance added to the family via marriage. They were exuberant but a trifle bossy. She smiled in the darkness, ruefulness filling her. Somehow, she'd committed to a shopping trip to Dunedin tomorrow when she'd intended to pack up their belongings and leave Middlemarch for good.

One extra day wouldn't matter. She still had her plan.

Marsh pulled up in front of the farmhouse and she found it difficult not to compare their home with the Mitchells' place. In the daylight, the white paint peeling from the old timber, the sloping floorboards of the interior, drew the eye.

"You get the lights," he said. "Both the boys are asleep. I'll carry them inside."

"They had fun." It had been good seeing them playing with young Sylvie, and even better, they'd behaved.

"I think we all enjoyed the outing."

Caroline sensed him looking in her direction, despite her lack of clear vision. Clouds shrouded the half-moon, the nip in the air promising the arrival of winter. "The Mitchells are a lovely family."

"They are. I used to spend time there after school if Mum and Dad were busy. That's when their Uncle Herbert was still alive. He took over after their parents died."

"He did a good job." Caroline hurried up the three uneven steps to the front door and pushed it open. She reached for the light. Illumination filled the doorway, then a loud pop sounded as the bulb died a violent death. "Great. We're out of replacement bulbs."

"Doesn't matter. My night vision is good," Marsh said. "Caroline, do we have any of that hot chocolate left? I wondered if we could talk once the boys are in bed."

Tension gripped her without warning. She didn't want to talk any longer, not when she'd come to a decision. She opened her mouth to say no, then decided she owed him the courtesy of an adult discussion. "Will milo do?" The malty chocolate drink was one of the few food items left in the cupboard. If she intended to stay another day, they'd need to shop for food. A problem since they had no money in the check account.

"Perfect," he said, his tone warm with approval.

She went mushy inside, hungry for every scrap of affection. Marsh, he'd swept her off her feet, and she still loved him. It was their situation—the constant battle to live and Marsh's long hours, his family's lack of warmth and charity that made their marriage so hard. The worst thing—she couldn't see this changing, which was why she'd decided to leave. She'd force change on them, breaking up their small family in the process.

"I'll help Ricky into his pajamas while you get James," she said.

"All right."

Ten minutes later, she'd settled both boys—angelic and fast asleep. Caroline bustled around the kitchen with nerves simmering in the pit of her stomach. Not difficult to discern the topic of discussion. Finally, with the milo ready she had no reason not to join him at the kitchen table they used to eat their meals.

Marsh took a sip of his milo and set the chunky mug down again. "I don't want you to go." He met her gaze, his own troubled. "I know things need to change. We're broke and never have time together as a family or as husband and wife. My parents—" He shrugged. "I love you, Caroline, and I want another chance to prove that we're good together."

His words held passion and strength, but she couldn't see change and said as much.

He pulled a face. "You're right. Our lives won't change if we stay here. What if we left Middlemarch?"

Caroline gaped at him, blinking rapidly as she replayed his words. Had she heard right?

He reached over to tap her chin with his forefinger, and she pressed her lips together. "Don't look so shocked. Saber told me Cam Sinclair, Saul's uncle—you remember Saul?"

At her nod, he continued.

"Cam Sinclair runs a sheep and cattle station in the Mackenzie country. He is looking for a farmhand. Saber said if I wanted the job he'd put a word in for me. I need to decide tonight because they're advertising the job soon."

"The Mackenzie? The stations in that region are remote."

"Cam's property is remote. According to Saber, they employ at least a dozen employees, some of them married with kids. One of the wives is a teacher, and she runs the correspondence school. Most of the time, they run regular work hours, except during lambing season. Part of the package is you helping with cooking, and they'd pay you for that. Saber gave me Cam's number and we can ring him tomorrow morning. What do you think? Could we try again? Start again somewhere new?"

"You'd do that? Leave Middlemarch, your family and friends?"

"We'd have a regular income we could count on and I'd get time off to spend with you and the boys. I spoke with Felix since he worked there for six months. He said Cam was a fair boss, and apart from busy times of the year, his men do have a regular schedule."

"Why did Felix leave if he liked the job so much?"

"Someone was stalking Tomasine, and he wanted to keep her safe. That's all I know."

Caroline nodded, her mind busy. "Could I speak with this Cam Sinclair too?"

"We can do the interview on speaker phone. If you have questions, you can ask Cam yourself." His green eyes darkened as he gazed at her. "So you'll do this? Give our marriage a second chance?"

"I'll think about it. Talk to Mr. Sinclair and maybe Tomasine."

Marsh reached for her hands and squeezed them hard before releasing them. "Thank you, Caroline. Things haven't been right between us for a long time, but believe this. I do love you. I love our children, and I want to make this work."

"What time will you ring? Emily and Isabella talked me into a shopping trip. They're coming to pick me up at ten. I'm dropping the boys at school and kindy before they whisk me off to Dunedin. We're out of cash, and I need to buy food, otherwise we won't have dinner."

"Once we've spoken to Cam Sinclair, I'll hunt down Dad." Marsh said in a grim voice.

"I don't need any for shopping, but the cupboards are empty."

"I'll take care of it," Marsh said, and steely resolve settled in his expression, a feral look that marched a shiver across her skin.

"Thanks." A yawn forced her mouth open, and she rose. "Pardon. I'm tired."

"Caroline."

"Yes?"

"Can I sleep in our bed tonight? I'm tired too. I just want to hold you, feel close again. Please."

If he'd ordered her or forced his way into their bed after his lengthy absence, she might have objected, but his please cut her off at the knees. She nodded before her brain even caught up with the conversation.

Marsh looked relieved, and she could see the tension lift from his muscular frame. His shoulders relaxed, his smile bathing her with humor. He held out his hand, his fingers gentle as he clasped hers. "Let's grab some sleep. It's late, and we've had an eventful day."

Marsh clasped Caroline in his arms, the darkness a familiar friend since his feline sight gave him excellent night vision. He breathed in her sweet floral scent and his feline purred.

"You're making that strange noise."

"It's happiness. Stop wriggling."

She froze. "Why?"

He led with truth. "Because we haven't had sex for months, and my body is reacting to your presence."

"Oh." Her small voice brought another grin. "Your...everyone says I've put on weight. I didn't think you wanted me."

"Who is everyone?" he demanded, furious at them for doing a number on her confidence. Caroline had put on weight during her two pregnancies. She'd always been curvy, a fact that had drawn him to her. "Who is telling you you're fat?" He rolled, gripping her shoulders and giving her a shake. "Tell me. Who?"

She blinked, her blue eyes filling with unshed tears.

"Caroline."

"Your mother."

"My mother said you're fat?"

A slight nod her only reply.

"You are not overweight. I love your body." He shifted positions and let his rigid cock graze her thigh. "Does this feel like an uninterested male?"

"No, but we haven't—"

"I'll feel this way about you when I'm eighty. Most people gain a little weight as they age."

"You haven't."

"My job is more physical." And it was almost impossible for a feline shifter to pile on huge amounts of weight. Their bodies burned energy fast. If anything, he came in underweight because he didn't eat enough.

"If we take this job, we'll spend more time together as a family. We'll be able to go swimming and walking. Teach the boys how to fly a kite. We can do fun things together. Remember how much we used to walk in Dunedin?"

"Until our hands and feet went numb with the cold, then we'd find a cheap café and buy a hot drink. I remember."

"Caroline, my parents won't take this well. Would you be happy for the boys to learn by correspondence? Felix said the kids range in age and they spend the morning together in the schoolroom. He said the teacher is excellent and Sylvie did well. She and the other mothers supervise the children in the afternoon, and they do arts and crafts and play games."

"I'll talk to Tomasine after our phone call."

"All right. Just so you know—I've pretty much decided to take this job. Felix said they loved life at the station but missed Middlemarch and their family. The Mitchells are close. It's easy to see their genuine affection for each other."

"This Cam Sinclair is a fair boss?"

"Yes. Felix said he had no problems with the work and Cam was fair. He liked the other employees and said most of them had been at the station for years. That says something."

"It does."

"Maybe I'll give Tomasine a quick call as soon as we wake. Ask her if she liked station life."

Marsh kissed her brow. He wanted to do more, but sensed they needed to heal their rift first. He understood even if he disliked the situation.

"Marsh?" She sounded hesitant.

"What, kitten?"

She smiled. "You haven't called me that for ages."

"Then I've been remiss." He kept his tone light while inside he beamed. They'd talked more tonight than they had in months.

"Marsh, will you kiss me good night?"

"I just did."

"A real kiss." Her words hung in the air and speared him with a jolt of adrenaline.

"Anytime," he said and closed the distance between them.

Her lips were soft, her rush of breath smelling of mint. He tasted her, savored her and kept the kiss light, not traveling into carnal territory as his feline urged. When he lifted his head, they were both breathing heavily and his dick felt as if it might burst. He dragged in a gulp of air, then a second one. A purr erupted, and Caroline giggled, the soft gurgle welcome, even if it was at his expense.

"Thanks. I wanted to know if we still had the spark."

"Nothing to worry about in that department," he said, his tone dry. "What we have is an inferno."

Chapter 4

Opportunity

M arsh dared to hope. If they could laugh together, they could make their relationship work. He brushed her hair from her face and stared at her in the darkness. Beautiful. While she'd put on weight she looked healthy and he loved every inch of her. He'd be having words with his mother tomorrow after he spoke to his father. It wouldn't go well—neither of the discussions. His parents thought they knew what was best for him and the grandchildren they accepted because of their feline genes. But Caroline was the mother of his children, and that didn't mean they could treat her with disrespect.

"Why didn't you tell me my mother was giving you a hard time?"

"No point. She hurt me, but she's always maintained a distance. I'm used to it."

"I want you, have always wanted you, Caroline. Never doubt that."

A tiny frown puckered her brow, and he pressed a kiss to the spot.

"I've allowed outside factors to intrude. Give us six months. If the talk with Cam Sinclair goes well, and we move to the Mackenzie, it will be a new start. Give us a chance to become a family."

"If the talk goes well," Caroline promised.

Marsh relaxed. "I'm looking forward to making love to you again."

"I...I..." The tremor in her voice suggested where her mind had veered.

He fixed it in the way he knew would spell out the truth, one she might believe because there was no lack of desire on his side. He grasped her hand and placed it on his groin. His cock tightened at the heat from her hand, her startled intake of air. He grinned again, even though his feline struggled for dominance.

She kept her hand on his dick when he'd thought she'd laugh and roll onto her side to go to sleep. Instead, her fingers flexed, and the squeeze reverberated through his body. His feline stretched beneath his skin and reacted with a speed Marsh hadn't experienced since the first time he'd met Caroline. Canines pushed free, piercing his gums. Claws forced their way beneath his fingernails, visible to him even in the darkness of their bedroom. He swallowed, his heart racing. *Don't shift. Don't shift. Don't shift.* He forced his mind to thoughts of frigid showers, rolling in the snow, mustering stock under the hard pelt of winter sleet.

Saber was right.

Caroline had deserved the truth about felines and the feline community in the early days of their marriage.

Now wasn't the right time.

If they moved to the high country station—he'd tell her then when she couldn't walk away.

Her fingers moved. A stroke.

"I thought you wanted to sleep."

"I never said that," Caroline said, and this time he was left in no doubt.

"Be sure, because I won't stop. I'll take this as a sign you want this marriage and will meet me halfway to fix our problems."

The hand stilled, and she crawled over his naked body, her heavy flannel pajamas dragging against his torso. "I want this."

"Define this."

She bit her bottom lip, torturing it with the drag of her teeth as she hesitated. "I've missed sex."

"Caroline, if this continues, I'm going to leap to conclusions. I don't want them to be the wrong ones."

She repeated the move with her lip, chewing it until he wanted to shout with frustration. He forced himself to stay silent, to wait.

"It depends on what happens tomorrow. I can't carry on the way we've been going, living so near your parents."

"What else are you keeping from me?"

She sighed. "They put me down in front of the boys. I've tried to ignore the comments, but my patience is shredded. I'd hate to cause a rift with your family."

Anger pumped through him and a feline growl squeezed through his flattened lips. She stilled, her eyes rounding and her hand jerked from his body. He missed her touch at once.

"My brother's death broke my parents. Angus was the golden child, four years older than me. He did everything they wanted without argument. He was bright and talented and they blame me for his death. I came as a surprise when they didn't think they'd have more children."

"Didn't you tell me he died in a motor vehicle accident? Your parents never mention him."

"He's there in the background, hovering like an apparition," Marsh said. "They compared us all the time. I didn't measure up well compared to Angus."

"Why do they blame you? You've never talked about your brother."

"Angus was teaching me to drive. I made a mistake at a stop sign and hit the accelerator instead of the brake. We drove into the path of another vehicle. Angus died instantly and the driver of the other vehicle stayed in the hospital for three weeks. I escaped injury." He shook his head, recalling his shock, his remorse and for the thousandth time wished he could go back to fix his mistake.

"Oh Marsh. That's terrible. How old were you?"

"Sixteen. Angus had just finished telling me off for not paying proper attention, but I was so excited to learn to drive. We were practicing on the back roads that seldom had traffic. On that day, the guy was in a hurry, speeding, late to an appointment."

"I'm so sorry. I can't imagine what you must have gone through."

"Time has made it a little easier, plus Sid Blackburn saw the entire accident from the paddock on the hill above the road. He told the cops I wasn't going fast, but I was driving and didn't stop. My parents have never forgiven me."

"I wondered about the tension. I thought your parents didn't approve of me."

"That's part of it. I've tried and you've tried. It's time to stop paying for a mistake and move on with our future."

Caroline's hand traveled across his biceps and up to his shoulder, her touch soothing his inner angst. Memories. Until the day of the accident, his recollections of his parents and brother had been good ones. Things changed.

"I think I've spoiled the mood."

Marsh gave in to the impulse to kiss her—a quick brush of lips. Then, he wrapped his arms around her, shifting his position to align their bodies. "I think honest discussion is more important. We don't take the time to talk. We've got out of the habit of doing lots of things and let our marriage drift."

"That's true." She snatched another kiss, this one lingering. She drew back and smiled. "We should try to sleep. It will be a busy day tomorrow."

"All right." Disappointment seared him, even as he understood. Their peace was too fragile yet, too new. He needed to move with caution. "I'll seduce you tomorrow night," he whispered. "Once we've made our decision."

"Is that a promise?"

A purr of satisfaction escaped him. "Tomorrow," he repeated, and he pulled her against his chest, wrapping his arms around her. "Maybe tomorrow you could ditch the pajamas. I'll take on the responsibility of keeping you warm."

The phone dragged Marsh from a deep sleep—the best rest he'd had for weeks.

"What is it?" a sleepy voice asked.

"Phone. It's early. Just gone six. Stay in bed." Marsh slid from the warmth and tucked the covers around Caroline. Her eyelids fluttered, and her breathing deepened.

The phone continued to ring, and Marsh dug in his jeans pocket. He glanced at the screen and muttered a low curse. Ignore. After placing his phone on vibrate, he set it aside. He'd dress first and grab a coffee, if they had any instant left in the cupboard, before he faced his father.

By the time he'd donned a worn T-shirt, a flannel shirt and a pair of faded jeans, his phone danced across the dresser. He scooped it up and strode toward the kitchen. "What do you want, Dad?"

"The cattle are gone."

"Which cattle?" Marsh pulled on a pair of socks and scoured the cupboard for a jar of coffee.

"The ones you shifted to the farm paddock yesterday. Didn't you shut the gate? At least half of them are gone."

"I shut the gate," Marsh said in a flat voice. "I'll check the fence and see if I can find them." He ended the call with a feline snarl. No coffee this morning. He'd make do with a glass of water.

When he arrived at the gate, he found it shut. The hoofprints at the gateway told Marsh the cattle had come out the gate, but someone had closed it again. He'd driven the cattle through the far gate on the other side of the paddock, so there shouldn't be prints in this gateway. Footprints covered the ground outside the gate, the wavy patterns not a match to his boots. He dragged in a lungful of air and caught an out-of-place scent. A stranger. He followed the tracks and the scent and came to tracks made by a vehicle. Someone had loaded stock onto a truck. Holes in the gravel road told him what happened.

Thieves had driven the cattle from the paddock, herded them into mobile yards and trucked them away.

Crap. Just what he needed today.

He pulled out his phone and rang his father.

"Well?"

"Someone loaded them on a truck."

"Someone stole them?"

"That's what it looks like."

"Fuck," his father growled.

"I'll ring the cops," Marsh said. "I'll wait for them to see the scene."

"Fat lot of use that will do. Hannah should've retired years ago."

"We need to go through the process," Marsh said, straining for patience. "At least that way we should be able to claim insurance."

"I didn't renew the policy."

"Why—never mind. I'll talk to you later." He disconnected and made his call to the police.

Hannah arrived ten minutes later and took down the details as Marsh showed him everything he'd noticed.

"I'll talk to the neighbors. Ask if they saw anything strange last night."

"Haven't other farmers reported missing stock?" Marsh asked.

"A small herd went missing two days ago, on the other side of Middlemarch. The same setup."

"Our cattle all wore our electronic ear tags. They won't be able to sell them, not through legitimate channels."

"I have the word out with the stock agents and the auctions. The police at Cromwell are receiving reports of missing stock too."

Marsh nodded. "I'd heard that other areas farther south had problems."

Jason Hannah rubbed his belly then adjusted his trousers, hauling them higher on his hips. "'Tis an epidemic."

"You'll ring me if you learn anything?"

The cop nodded and plodded back to his vehicle.

Marsh scowled after him, not holding much hope. Hannah and the other cop at Middlemarch were a joke, going through the motions and hanging on until they reached retirement age. Locals were still discussing the two mystery bodies that turned up in the area. One body disappeared while en route to Dunedin and no one had seen a thing.

Marsh jogged to his parents' house to report on the stock in person. Damn, that had taken longer than he'd expected. By the time he finished with his father, he'd be cutting it short to make the eight o'clock phone call. He pulled up and rang Caroline.

"Caroline, it's Marsh." He explained what had happened. "If I don't make it back by eight, can you ring Cam and do the interview? You know what we want to learn. The wages, the hours, where we'll be living, the duties for both of us. Anything else? Maybe make a list so we forget nothing. If I don't make it back, explain what has happened and give my apologies. Ask if we can ring him with a decision." He paused. "No, if you think it sounds as if the position will work for me, accept the job. He'll speak with Saber. He'll know I'm capable of doing the work."

"You'd trust me to make the final decision?" Surprise tinged her voice.

"I trust you to do the best for us and the boys. You've never failed me yet. Hell, Dad looks as if he might burst. Gotta go. I'll try to get back in time. Love you."

C aroline kept one eye on the clock while she made a late breakfast for the boys. The digital numbers ticked over, moving closer to eight. She mentally rescheduled her day, adding in a school run because they'd missed the bus. If the phone call went longer than an hour, James would be late to school.

She sat and jotted several questions on a notepad, things she thought Marsh would want to know. Stock numbers. Mix of stock. Other employees. Terms and conditions. Wages. Time off. Things she wanted to know. Her duties. Wages. Accommodation. School for the boys. Expenses included in the wage package.

The phone peeled, and she wiped her palms on her track pants. Nerves. A reminder of the phone call she needed to make soon. After speaking with Marsh she wanted this chance to move forward with their marriage.

She picked up the phone.

"Caroline, it's Emily. Just wanted to confirm that we'll pick you up at ten. Is that still all right?"

"That's fine," Caroline said.

"Something wrong?"

"Someone stole a herd of cattle last night, and Marsh is caught up with the aftermath. I need to make a phone call to Mr. Sinclair, and I'm nervous. Hopefully, the call won't take too long because I have to drive James to school."

"I'll be there in ten minutes," Emily said. "I'm checking in at the café before we leave to make sure my helpers are set. Your place is on the way. If you're okay with the idea, I can take James to school and your youngest can come with me to the café."

"Are you sure?"

"I'm driving past your place anyway."

"Thank you. That would be a huge help. Ricky isn't good at remaining quiet for ten minutes, let alone half an hour."

"You'll be fine. You have a list? I live my life with my lists. Saber and the others always tease me."

Caroline laughed, feeling in charity with the bubbly woman. "I've just written mine."

"See you soon."

Caroline organized the two boys and after Emily arrived, she transferred car seats and buckled in her sons.

"We're dressing for comfort for this shopping trip. I'm wearing this." Emily gestured at her jeans and blouse before she climbed back into the driver's seat.

"Comfort is good."

"We'll pick you up at ten. Good luck with your job interview."

"Thanks." Caroline waved to her sons and Emily as they drove away.

"Where is she taking my grandsons?" Dawn asked in an icy tone.

Caroline tensed, sucked in a quick breath and turned to face her mother-in-law. "Emily Mitchell is dropping James at school and looking after Ricky for an hour while I take care of stuff here."

"What sort of stuff? Why didn't you ask me to look after Ricky?"

Caroline fought to remain silent. Dawn refused to mind Ricky unless it suited her. "Emily offered."

"Why do you need privacy?"

"I promised to make a new dress." Caroline chose to lie rather than tell her mother-in-law of the prospective job. "Ricky can't sit still this week." She stopped talking and glanced at her watch. "I must go."

"Wait. I need you to cook a cake for me to take to a party. You're so much better at it than me."

"I'm sorry, but I'm too busy to bake today."

"Why?"

"I'm going out for the day."

Dawn frowned. "Where are you going? You don't have friends."

Bitch. Caroline bit back another retort, one that might be taken as rude. She refused to stoop to the levels of her mother-in-law. "I'm sorry, Dawn." And she turned and walked inside their house, shutting the door behind her.

Two steps toward the kitchen, her door flew open. "If you're going shopping, who is looking after the children?"

"Marsh."

"Marsh will be working. He can't look after children."

"Marsh said he could. Is that all? I need to get moving." Without waiting for a reply, Caroline turned and strode to the kitchen. It felt as if Dawn glared holes in her back, and she was glad when she heard the retreat of her mother-in-law's footsteps, then the thump of the door closing.

She glanced at the clock to check the time. Two minutes to the hour. Good enough. She wiped her palms again and reached for the phone.

Chapter 5

Changes

"**Y**ou ungrateful brat."

Marsh stared at his father and wondered if he should try to apologize again for the teenage mistake that had broken their family. His hand rose to rub at the ache of regret pressuring his chest. They'd never been close, and after the accident... He missed Angus too, mourned his loss, had cried like a baby in private to avoid his father's scoffing. He'd loved his older brother, worshiped him, but now he had to move on with his life. Concentrate on his family, his responsibilities.

He forced himself to speak, to hasten this confrontation when he'd rather escape to the peacefulness of the land. "Dad, half the time you don't pay me. You owe me wages from months ago, and you expect me to work long hours. I have to beg for time off. Caroline and I can't keep living this way."

"You've allowed that mealy-mouthed human to sway your good sense," his father spat. "I told you no good would come from this union."

"You did," Marsh said. "I didn't listen then, and I won't now. Caroline and I are leaving Middlemarch."

Charles laughed, bitterness leaching the sound of humor. "Where will you go? No one will hire you. I won't give you a reference."

"That is why we're leaving," Marsh said. "Goodbye, Dad. Do you want us to stop by before we leave so you can say goodbye to James and Ricky?"

"Don't bother," Charles roared, his feline rushing to the surface.

Marsh stood his ground, meeting his father's fury without flinching. "I've made my decision."

"Who will work the farm?"

"Hire someone. Dad, I need my wages. Can you give me cash today?"

Charles snorted, his face contorting into mean and ugly. "You have got to be kidding me. If you're running out on me, you're not getting a cent."

"I've earned those wages."

"You let someone steal a hundred head of cattle. That was your wages."

Marsh studied his father for long seconds. There was no softening in his expression, no compassion. "Goodbye Dad. Have a nice life."

D awn's left hand gripped her phone. "Valerie, I thought the council might help us. Marsh is leaving and taking the boys with him." She paced the length of her designer kitchen. "Of course he's taking the human with him. This is where the problem started. If he'd kept his pants zipped…"

"Your son is an adult," Valerie said. "We can't force him to do anything."

"I thought you'd talk sense into him. We didn't want him to leave."

Valerie remained silent for a time, then her heavy exhalation echoed down the line. "Have you talked to him? Explained your position?"

The unspoken censure had Dawn's feline snarling, pacing her mind. "Numerous times. He shouldn't have married that woman."

"You love your grandchildren. You wouldn't have grandchildren if it wasn't for Caroline."

"Marsh could have married the McCulloh girl or the Kirkpatrick girl. He dated both of them while attending varsity in Dunedin. Then, the next thing Charles and I knew, Marsh brought Caroline home, told us she was pregnant, and they intended to get married. He didn't even discuss the matter. At least we persuaded him not to tell her about our feline status. Imagine the mess we'd be in if she knew."

"Why? Other humans know of our existence. They are loyal to our community. You should have told Caroline the truth. They've been together for what...almost six years?"

"It's her fault. She is making Marsh do this, leaving Charles in the lurch on the farm."

Valerie made agreeing sounds, dampening down Dawn's agitation.

"So you'll speak with the council again?"

"Our next meeting is this afternoon. Do you know where Marsh is going?"

"No, he refused to tell us. He said he wanted a fresh start and time to settle in before he contacted us again. He...Charles and Marsh had words. Charles doesn't wish to see Marsh, but I want to see my grandchildren."

"I understand," Valerie said in a crisp, no-nonsense tone. "I'll be in touch."

The next morning, Caroline placed her hands on her hips and glared at the overflowing suitcases. "How are we going to fit everything into the car? We can't afford to hire a moving van to get our stuff to the Mackenzie."

"I'll talk to my parents," Marsh said. "They might let us store some of our stuff."

She wrinkled her nose. Dawn and Charles never did anything the easy way, and since Marsh had told his parents they were leaving, his father had gone out of his way to make things difficult. "I can't believe he's threatening to chuck us out of our house."

"Or not. I didn't say it would be easy. Dad is still refusing to give me the wages he owes me."

"What are we going to do, Marsh? We haven't got any food in the cupboards. The boys ate the last of the breakfast cereal this morning. We have five days to go before we're due at Glenshee Station. We need money to buy petrol for the journey and food until we go—" She broke off with a helpless shrug, tears filling her eyes. She could do without food, but the boys...it wasn't fair. "Your parents keep saying how they love their grandchildren and want them to stay, but they're making them suffer."

Marsh went to her and wrapped his arms around her trembling body. "Shush, kitten. It will be all right."

She pulled back and rubbed the back of her neck. "How?"

She couldn't see anything but stress in their coming days. Things were bad enough now. James had asked her what was wrong this morning before she'd walked him to the school bus. How could she tell him that his beloved grandparents were the source of her anxiety? And that she'd been crying because she'd found five-dollars in change down the back of the couch.

"I'll think of something."

"We could sell my jewelry—the necklace my grandmother gave me."

"No. Absolutely not. Let me go and see my parents one final time."

"And what about our stuff?"

"I'm sorry, kitten, but we'll have to restrict ourselves to clothes and important items. Just the things we can fit into the car. Bedding. Towels. Clothing. Toiletries. Get the boys to choose their favorite toys and books."

She let out a huff and stared at her feet before meeting his gaze again. "Okay. Should I start packing the car now?"

"Might as well. It might be easier while the boys are at school and kindy." Marsh glanced at his watch. "I'll stop by my parents' place, then come back to help you pack." His hands tightened on her shoulders. "Hey."

A long, low cry escaped, burning her tight throat as it emerged. "I feel so helpless. I rang my parents, intending to ask them for money, but I couldn't. They're saving for a holiday, the first they've had for years. It didn't feel right to ask, even though I know they would've given it to us."

"You shouldn't have to ask. This is my fault."

No. No, it wasn't. It was his parents trying to wreak havoc and pull them apart. Marsh had earned those wages, and it wasn't as if they were asking for money they weren't owed.

"If your father refuses to give us the money he owes us, make sure he knows that we can't afford to buy food to feed our children."

His father's farm vehicle was parked in front of the house when Marsh walked up their driveway. He knocked on the door and waited for his mother to answer his summons. When the door opened, he forced a smile, determined to keep his temper and act with dignity. Remain calm.

"Mother."

"Marsh, thank goodness you've come to your senses. If you apologize to your father, he'll give you your job back. I understand you're attached to Caroline, but it's better if you part ways. Come inside. Talk to your father. We'll sort everything out and fix this slight upset."

He blinked rapidly and remained rooted in the doorway. Fuck, they truly expected him to walk away from Caroline. She was his mate, yet they didn't support either of them in their relationship.

"I've come for my wages."

"I told the boy he lost my cattle. I don't owe him any wages," his father shouted from the other room. With his feline hearing, he hadn't missed a thing.

Marsh drew in a sharp breath, fought to rein in his temper. His father had started spreading rumors about Marsh and Caroline around the district. The local feline gossip vine pulsed and glowed with tidbits and falsehoods, malicious rumors perpetrated by his parents. He ground his molars together and glared at his mother. "We don't have money. Don't you care that the boys won't have dinner?"

He caught the flash of concern in his mother before his father appeared behind her.

"Not our problem. You've made your decision, and now you live with it." His voice was harsh, his words dripping with scorn, and Marsh realized he was wasting his breath.

He turned and walked away, heard the firm clunk of the door as it closed. *Bastard*. All he cared about was his precious pride. He expected Marsh to follow his orders without argument. Marsh stomped back toward their farm cottage, only slowing when his phone vibrated in his pocket. He halted and glanced at the screen.

"Hi, Saber."

"I heard you took the job."

"Yeah, I start in five days."

"Problem?"

"We don't have any money or food." Embarrassment warmed his cheeks at the confession. "I doubt we can scrape together enough money for the petrol."

"Come and stay with us," Saber said without hesitation. "We have plenty of room. Or, if you don't want to do that, give Cam a call. I'm sure he won't mind if you go early. Think about it, but meantime, come for dinner."

"Are you sure? You've been so good to us already. I don't want to put you to any trouble."

"It's no trouble," Saber said. "I'll see you at six."

"Thanks." Marsh disconnected and placed the phone in his pocket. Saber's idea about them going earlier than they'd planned was a good one. All they needed to figure out was the petrol money. He strode up their driveway and found

SHELLEY MUNRO

Caroline outside, packing blankets into the car. "Saber invited us to dinner tonight. What do you think about going to the Mackenzie earlier? Tomorrow if we can swing it."

"Could we do that?"

"I'll ring Cam now. Actually, it might be better if we could go early. I wouldn't put it past Dad to make good on his threat to kick us out."

A furrow creased Caroline's brow and her expression turned grim. "Did you get money?"

"Not yet, but don't worry. I will. I'll wear down my father. You'd better not pack anything else into the car yet since we're going to the Mitchells for dinner. We'll finish packing once we get home." He picked up the landline phone and rang Cam. A few minutes later, he hung up and went to find Caroline. "Cam said our cottage is ready for us now. It's no trouble if we arrive tomorrow." One problem fixed. Marsh swallowed hard. Time to move on to the more pressing one of money. "Have you started packing our room yet?"

"No, not yet."

"I'll make a start. Shout if you need me for anything."

In their bedroom, Marsh pulled out his cell phone, his shoulders slumping momentarily before he straightened with determination. They needed money. He sucked in a quick breath to calm his racing pulse and hit speed dial.

86

"Are we there yet?" James asked from the rear seat.

Marsh grinned at Caroline before replying. "Not long now, kiddo. We'll stop at Lake Tekapo to let you run off energy. I think we can spring for a coffee for us and milkshakes since we won't be near a café for a few weeks."

"Can we afford it?" Caroline asked.

Marsh coughed. "The—yes." He sucked in a quick breath as if he required fortification then spoke fast. "Saber loaned me five hundred dollars when I asked him. I—we—are paying it back at twenty dollars per week. Dad refused—I felt embarrassed, and I should have told you when it happened. Dad...I'm sorry."

Caroline watched the ruddy color creep into the tips of his ears and understood his reluctance to inform her of this latest debacle with his parents. It can't have been easy dealing with the crap his parents had pulled this week. The rumors. The nastiness. She reached over and placed her hand on his left where it rested on the steering wheel. "We've had a stressful week, so I'll give you a pass this time. If I can make items to sell at the market, we should pay the money back soon enough. I gave Isabella several kids' shirts and dresses I've made. Most are secondhand, but she said she'd try to sell them at the upcoming market. I figured it was better to sell them than leave them in storage."

"That was a good idea." Marsh's glance held gratefulness for her easy acceptance. "Thanks."

"Don't forget to tell me stuff again. You don't get a second pass."

"Noted. James, if you look closely, you should be able to see Lake Tekapo soon."

"I see it, Daddy."

"Me too. Me too," Ricky cried.

Caroline smiled, taken by the vibrant glacier blue of the lake. "It's beautiful. I don't remember the lake being such a pretty blue although it's fifteen years since I came here with my parents for a holiday."

"I want to draw it," James said.

"Not today," Marsh said. "We're having a quick stop, but we'll come back to visit. We can swim in the hot pools, and if it's cold enough, we can try ice skating."

"I'll take photos and you can draw from those," Caroline suggested. "Do you think you have crayons the right color blue?"

James frowned in concentration, and she saw Marsh in him then. Marsh drew his brows together in that way when he was pondering a weighty problem.

"Why don't I take Ricky to buy the coffee and milkshakes while you and James take photos? Once we get back, we can sit by the lake for a while."

"Sounds good." She and James set off to find the perfect spot to take photos, and she turned to find Marsh ogling her butt. Her mouth dropped open. Heat rushed to her cheeks followed by pleasure that she'd caught him looking. Instinct had her winking. "Later, Mr. Rutherford."

"Count on it, Mrs. Rutherford."

"Can we go across that bridge?" James asked, pointing to a footbridge spanning a river that ran into the lake. On the other side, tourists in rental cars and camper vans jostled for parking spaces near the small stone church that sat on the lakeshore.

"Not this time, sweetie. We have more driving before we arrive at our new house. Are you excited? I'm excited about trying something new."

"Grandma said you're kidnapping us. She wanted to know where we were going."

Caroline cursed under her breath. She'd done a lot of that this week, and she hadn't been the only one in the family cursing a blue streak. In fact, Cam Sinclair deserved a big kiss for letting them move to the station early. He'd helped them out of a huge jam.

A new life.

"Over there, Mum," James said, taking her hand and dragging her to the edge of the rocky shoreline. "I want to paint the lake from here with the brown hills and mountains and the funny clouds."

Obligingly, she snapped a photo of the glacier-blue lake, the dry, barren hills surrounding the lake. Clouds sat in a dip between the hills, fluffy and white and intriguing. Caroline took several photos with her small camera.

"That might be enough." She turned to glance in the direction they'd walked from and saw Marsh. He held their drinks in a carrier as he herded Ricky past two seagulls sitting on the tarmac.

A group of tourists—teenagers—eyed Marsh as he wandered past. He didn't glance in their direction or notice their giggles and speculation. As he neared her and James, his grin widened.

"Did I tell you how much I like you in that color? It brings out the blue of your eyes." He tapped her nose. "But you'll grow more freckles if we don't get out of this sun."

The teenagers slowed as they passed them, but Marsh had eyes for no one except her. A real confidence boost.

At Glenshee Station, one of the workers guided them to their allocated housing. Their new home wasn't spacious—a wooden bungalow with two single bedrooms and one double. The kitchen, however, was an improvement. Part of a big open space, it took up one corner. The central island, featuring cupboard storage and a counter worktop perfect for breadmaking, separated the food preparation area from the dining and living space.

Caroline turned to Marsh, a little breathless with excitement. This was so much better than she'd anticipated and a step—heck, two steps up from their Middlemarch residence. "It's perfect for the kids. I can work in the kitchen and still supervise them while they're playing. They can have their own bedrooms."

"If that means I get to sleep with you, I'm in favor of that plan."

Caroline inhaled the fresh, crisp air of the higher altitude and met Marsh's gaze. Her mind sauntered straight to sex, and it became difficult to ignore the tiny patter of butterflies in the pit of her stomach. In the end, they'd slept in the same bed but hadn't done more than cuddle and kiss. Marsh told her he wanted her, touched her as if he did, but the lack of lovemaking worried her a little.

"We're starting over again. A fresh beginning. This means in all facets of our lives." At least, she'd strung words—the right reply—together.

Marsh swooped on her, grasped her in his arms and kissed her. Not the affectionate peck he'd bestowed on her for most of this week. This was a kiss indicating he meant business, and he took his time, leaving her breathless and dazzled and more than a little turned on.

"I'm never gonna kiss a girl." James pulled a face and hid his eyes with spread fingers.

Caroline felt Marsh's splutter of laughter against her lips and chuckled herself once she could breathe.

Marsh continued to hold her in a loose embrace and grinned at his son. "You never know. You might change your mind. Ginny Kirkpatrick kissed me when I was your age. She kissed me at every opportunity. My friends teased me and I skulked around the playground because I never knew when Ginny would try to surprise me."

James peeked, saw they'd stopped kissing and nodded his head emphatically. "Karen Jones wanted one of us to kiss her. We said no."

"Did you tell the teacher?" Caroline asked.

"Yes." Another nod. "She had to sit in the corner for the whole afternoon."

Marsh shared an amused glance with her, his sexy lips twitching. "Lucky we've moved. When you get older you might want to kiss a girl. I like to kiss your mother." He lowered his voice. "I'm looking forward to doing other things with you later tonight."

Caroline studied the wicked expression in his eyes. Her tongue came out to moisten dry lips and his pupils dilated. "I...I'm looking forward to that." Nothing less than the truth. Marsh thought she was beautiful. He'd touched her constantly during the last few days. In private, he'd kissed her, slipped his hand over her backside. In public, he'd slid his arm around her waist or placed his hand in the small of her back to guide her. She'd noticed her father-in-law's sneer when they'd met him at the petrol station. It had been hard not to, but at least she understood now that her in-laws believed Marsh had killed his brother.

Not that she approved of their behavior.

A knock sounded on the door. "Hello," a voice called.

Marsh opened the door to an older man with a full head of gray hair. His tanned face and the network of wrinkles spoke of a life spent outdoors but his smile held warmth and welcome. "Mr. Sinclair?"

"I told you on the phone. Everyone calls me Cam. You must be Caroline." He offered his hand to both of them. "I'm pleased to have you here. Saber spoke well of you both, and I value his opinion. We're having an informal get together up at the main house. Since it's Sunday we try to take care of just the basic chores and let most of the men have the day off. Did you need any help with unloading?"

"We've got it," Marsh said. "We have our clothes and a few personal possessions."

"All right. Come when you're ready. Some of the workers have arrived. The kids are playing on the lawn and making the most of the fine weather." He lifted his head to sniff the air. "It won't last much longer. Think we'll have an early snowfall this year."

"Thank you, Mr.—Cam," Caroline said, taking an instant liking to the big man.

"Can we have a few words about the roster for this week?" Cam asked.

"I'll organize the boys," Caroline said.

She headed back inside and unpacked the boys' clothes. Each of the single rooms had a built-in dresser and a wardrobe. The walls bore evidence of the earlier inhabitant, the bits of tape and pin holes indicating lots of posters. Cam had said they could paint or redecorate if they wanted. Maybe in their room and the lounge, but the boys might like to have posters.

"James, come and help me unpack your clothes and toys please."

James appeared in the doorway. "The air smells different here."

Caroline tucked underwear in a drawer. "Lots of things are different here. This is your room. We will meet the other people who live on the station soon, but you have time to unpack your books and toys. You can keep them in the bottom drawers. Okay?"

By the time Marsh came back inside, she'd made the three beds and started unpacking Marsh's clothes. Marsh was frowning.

"Problem?"

"No, it's a lot to take in. Glenshee Station is so big. They have a helicopter to muster the high country. I can have my own dogs if I want."

"Could we get a dog for the boys?"

"I think that will be all right. Let's settle in first and discuss the pet issue later. Are you ready to go?"

"Sure thing." Caroline glanced at her rumpled dress, an attack of nerves at meeting new people and wanting to fit in so badly doing a number on her confidence. "Do you think I need to change?"

"Cam said it's casual. Let's go as we are. I'll round up the troops."

M arsh hurried away, his mind on his conversation with Cam. Saber had informed Cam that Caroline didn't know about shifters. Cam had said he'd told everyone, but he expected Marsh to fill Caroline in sooner rather than later.

He knew Cam was right.

But revealing his true self terrified him.

Their relationship still teetered, and he thought he'd die if Caroline left him.

Then there was the fact their sons were feline since feline genes trumped human ones in the gene pool.

Aware that he needed honesty, he'd discussed this with Cam. Cam had given him a month. He said, and Marsh agreed, that the men who worked for him loved life at the station because they could change at whim. They shouldn't have their lives disrupted because he worried about his human wife's reaction.

"We're ready," Caroline said with a bright smile. She'd loosened her hair from the practical ponytail and colored her mouth with lipstick.

He closed the distance between them and pressed a kiss to the top of her head. "You look stunning." He clasped her hand. "Ready, boys? I'll point out the new places as we go."

James trotted ahead, Ricky following with his usual determination.

"Ricky is flagging," Caroline said.

"We don't have to stay for long, but it's important to meet everyone."

"I'm nervous."

Marsh glanced at her. "Me too."

They both laughed at that and walked up the wide gravel road to the main homestead. They passed several other houses that looked much like theirs. Some had gardens full of vivid-colored flowers while other lawns bore discarded toys.

"There aren't many trees in the Mackenzie basin," Caroline said.

"Not the place to come if you want to learn to climb trees," Marsh agreed.

They rounded a bend, and the homestead came into view.

"Wow, it's like something out of a magazine," Caroline breathed, and Marsh heard the awe in her voice.

"Felix told me Cam's grandparents built the house. They've added on as the years have passed."

"Who does the gardens?"

"Both Cam and his wife enjoy growing things."

Greenery contrasted with splashes of orange, yellow and red. A wide verandah supported hanging baskets filled with purple and white petunias. With his feline hearing, Marsh could hear the casual chatter and the shrieks of playing children.

A small boy ran into sight and as Marsh opened a white gate, he disappeared around the corner.

"The new people are here," he shouted.

Marsh grinned and a glance at his sons told him they'd heard too. "This way," he said, guiding Caroline to a path that ran around the house.

"How do you know?"

"That's where the people are," James said, answering for Marsh.

"I swear you have the hearing of bats," Caroline said. "I can't hear anything. Maybe I should get my hearing checked?"

"There is nothing wrong with your hearing." James and Ricky ran around the corner. "Come on." Marsh tugged her after him, registered the tremor of her hand and stopped. He cupped her face. "Don't worry. They'll all love you, especially once they taste your cooking."

Chapter 6

Glenshee Station Welcome

C aroline allowed Marsh to tug her toward the cluster of strangers. She forced her shaky knees to bear her weight and toddled after him while praying she didn't trip. This was so important. She had to make a good impression, for Marsh's sake.

"Ah, good. You're here," Cam said. "I'll introduce you."

He led them from group to group, introducing them to everyone.

Both men and women were friendly, openly curious but made them welcome.

"Come and meet my wife," Cam said to Caroline. "Maria is in the kitchen. I figured you might like to see where you'll be working."

Cam ushered Caroline inside to a spacious living room. Antique furniture combined with more modern, comfortable pieces to produce a welcoming ambiance. Paintings of lakes and mountains covered part of one wall while several portraits stared at her with stern frowns from another. Her bare feet—bare since she'd insisted on removing her dusty shoes at the entrance—sank into the oatmeal-colored carpet.

"You have a beautiful house."

"Thank you. My Maria has turned it into a home." Affection shaded his voice as he led the way down a passage.

The scent of cooking drifted toward them. A roast of beef, by the delicious aroma.

"Maria, I've brought Caroline to meet you," Cam hollered as he strode through an open door.

Caroline followed, instantly dazzled by the huge modern kitchen. Silver appliances and a large central island of marble.

A tall woman with dark brown hair grinned at them, her capable hands mixing what looked like a batch of bread. "I am so pleased to meet you, Caroline. You have no idea. None of the other women enjoy cooking, so when I learned you're willing to step in and help me...color me thrilled."

"I love cooking. It was a bonus when Cam said he'd be willing to pay me for doing something I enjoy."

"I'll leave you alone to discuss tactics," Cam said. "Most of the staff are here."

"Righto. I'll bring out the snacks in ten minutes."

Cam disappeared and Maria seemed to shrivel in front of her eyes.

"Are you all right?"

"I think I'm coming down with the flu," Maria said. "I have no energy today."

"Sit. Let me do that for you. Have you taken anything?"

"A couple of tablets for my headache." Maria wavered on her feet and Caroline slipped her arm around the woman's waist.

"You should be in bed."

"Can't. Someone has to feed the single men."

"I can do it for you," Caroline said, and placed her hand on Maria's forehead. The woman had a temperature. "Tell me what you need doing. I'll make a list and take care of the evening meal. Do you make breakfast as well?"

"And packed lunches."

"Okay. Let me take care of this bread and you tell me what I need to do."

"Hard to concentrate with this headache."

"Why didn't you tell Cam you weren't well?"

"I didn't want to worry him."

"He'll worry more if you keel over."

"That I will," Cam boomed from the doorway. "Why didn't you tell me you were under the weather?" He cast an apologetic glance at Caroline. "Can you deal with the kitchen for Maria?"

"Yes. If I run into difficulties, I check with the men. They can tell me what Maria normally makes for them."

Cam nodded and scooped his wife off the wooden kitchen chair.

"There are snacks in the fridge for everyone. Cupcakes in the pantry for the kids," Maria called in a weak voice.

"I'll take care of it," Caroline promised.

Once Cam's footsteps receded, she stared around the kitchen, taking in the commercial appliances. She'd finish kneading the bread and set it to proof then sort out the snacks. Then, she'd interrogate the men outside to discover what she'd let herself in for.

Marsh met the other farm employees. Several were mated and had children. They lived in homes similar to the one allocated to them. Cam had told him all the cottages—that was what he called them—were the same to prevent arguments. There were six single men who lived in the big cottage. Maria cooked meals for them while the mated men ate at home with their families.

Glenshee Station, named after the Scottish town where Cam's forebears had lived before emigrating to New Zealand, hired more men than most—all shifters—apart from Caroline and Maria—which made Cam's advice to tell Caroline of the existence of feline shifters imperative.

Selfishly, he decided to leave it a couple of days longer. For the first time in months, he and Caroline were talking, flirting with each other, and he wanted that to reach its natural conclusion. Every muscle in his body tensed as he imagined making love with her, savoring her softness, her humor, the tiny noises she made when about to climax. Yeah. He sighed. Greedily, he wanted all that before he blasted their world off its axis again with the news he turned furry on a whim and their children would too.

Marsh kept glancing in the direction Caroline had gone.

Someone nudged him in the ribs and he jerked from his preoccupation.

"You have it bad for your lady," a petite woman with a mass of curly black hair said. "Have you not been together for long?" She leaned closer. "Cam told us she doesn't know a thing about shifters."

"Long story," Marsh said, his tone dry.

"But you have two children. Is this your second marriage?"

"No, as I said, a long story." Marsh smiled since he didn't intend to tell this woman their life story, despite her shifter status.

"Maria is a chatterer. I bet she's bending your lady's ear. I'm Josie, and you've met Alistair, my mate."

"I have."

"Go and check on her. I can see you're uneasy." Josie possessed a feline appearance with green slanted eyes and a snub nose. People would remark on it and come near the truth without knowing. "The kitchen is along the passage. You'll be able to follow the scent."

Marsh checked outside for the children. Ricky was playing a rough-and-tumble game with a group of boys while James was sitting with a girl of his age. They had crayons in their hands, their discussion intense, and Marsh grinned. This change would be good for the boys, no matter what his parents might say.

"The kids will be fine," Josie said with a nudge of her pointed chin. "We all keep watch." Her stomach grumbled. "I hope the food comes soon. Maria usually has us eating by now. She doesn't approve of drunken employees."

"Thanks," Marsh said. "Perhaps they've lost track of time."

"Then it's good you're going in search of your lady. Give them a reminder."

Marsh dragged in the scents, picked out Caroline's, and followed the trail along the passage. He strolled into a big kitchen, full of shiny appliances and a big center island. A working kitchen, for sure.

"Marsh, is everyone clamoring for food?"

"Where's Maria?"

"She's sick. Cam has taken her up to bed. I'm almost finished with this bread, then I can bring out the snacks."

Marsh studied her pink cheeks, the lock of hair that had fallen over her face and she kept blowing at to move. "Here. Let me." He tucked the curl behind her ear. "So you've been tossed in the deep end."

"Looks like."

"You okay?"

"I think so." She gave the bread a final pat and covered the bowl with a tea towel. After washing her hands, she went to the fridge then pantry. "Ah, everything is ready. I need to wheel these trolleys out. There should be cupcakes somewhere."

"Over there," he said pointing to another shelf in the large walk-in pantry. "I'll wheel this one out for you while you sort out the cupcakes."

"Are you sure?"

"Of course, I'm sure. I have no problem helping you."

"Your father—"

"Would have a tantrum about women's work. That's not me, Caroline. Dad isn't here. We are, and we're the ones who get to say how our life goes."

She stared at him with wide blue eyes, then nodded. "That would be a big help."

Heavy footsteps heralded Cam's arrival.

"How is Maria?" Caroline asked.

"Not so good. She insists she is fine, but I might drive her to the doctor. The closest practice is at Twizel."

Caroline frowned. "I thought you had someone here who does first aid."

Cam nodded. "Maria."

"Ah. I'd better get this food out," Caroline said. "Maria will rest easier if she knows everything is going smoothly in the kitchen."

"I appreciate your help," Cam said. "Can you sort out the evening meal for the single men too? Maria said she has a roast on the go. I know you're not due to start yet. I'll pay you for this."

"It's no problem," Caroline said. "I can wing it if I run into problems."

Cam nodded again, but his worry for his mate filled his expression. He grasped the handle of one tea trolley and wheeled it from the kitchen.

"The kids are fine. They're playing and the adults are watching them," Marsh said. "Shout if you need help." He kissed her cheek and wheeled out the other trolley.

Caroline followed with two plates of cupcakes.

"Where's Maria?" someone called.

"She's sick," Cam said.

Heads turned in concert, similar expressions of worry. These people cared about their employers, which boded well for her and Marsh and the boys.

"She rarely gets sick," an elderly man commented.

"No," Cam said with a frown. "I might check on her again."

"Set the cupcakes here," a petite woman with black curly hair suggested. "I'll supervise the hellions so they don't grab more than one each."

"Caroline, this is Josie," Marsh said.

"Kids, come and get a cupcake," Josie hollered, her boom a shock coming from the small frame.

The afternoon passed into evening, darkness falling and shrouding the mountainous landscape.

"You and the boys should come and eat with the single men," Cam said to Marsh. "We eat around six, and it smells as if Caroline has things on track."

The employees had drifted off to their homes, tired kids in tow.

"Ricky is asleep," Marsh said.

"No, he's not," Cam said with a rough laugh of amusement.

Marsh turned to see his youngest son sitting up and rubbing his eyes.

Caroline appeared. "The meal is almost ready and the men have arrived. They said they're capable of setting the table for me. I've made soup for Maria and prepared a tray. I thought she might like something light."

"Bless you," Cam said. "I'll tell the boys to set four extra places."

"Ricky had a sleep," Marsh said. "He seems wide awake now."

"I dreamed I was a cat," Ricky said. "I was black and had whiskers."

Caroline ruffled their son's hair. "That must have been exciting."

Marsh stared at Ricky, shock pummeling his chest. He'd dreamed of leopards a couple of years before his first shift—a sign predicting a shift and their people thought the dreams helped to prepare the body and mind for shifting.

"I drawed some cats," James said and thrust a paper at Marsh.

"You drew some cats," Marsh corrected. Another spear of shock struck him. James had drawn a big black leopard, two smaller ones and what looked like a lady with red hair. Mountains surrounded the figures on the page. "This is superb." He glanced at Caroline and saw her leading Ricky toward the kitchen. "Do you dream of cats too?"

"Sometimes," James said. "Other times I dream of pie. Pie is yummy."

Marsh laughed and ruffled his son's hair. "I like pie too. What is your favorite?"

"The peach and raspberry one Mummy made. Sylvie said she can change into a cat."

"She did?" Crap. This was not happening. Sylvie had shifted at five, unusual amongst their kind. Was it possible his two sons might shift early too? He needed to talk to someone. Cam. No, he had enough to worry about with Maria. Saber. He could ring Saber. "We'd better get ready for dinner. It smells good."

"Meat," James said. "I like meat."

"It's my favorite," Marsh agreed.

Marsh led his son to the dining room, off the kitchen, toward the rumble of men's voices. But his mind didn't dwell on food. It was on the huge problem that had just landed in his lap. If there was a chance of their sons shifting soon, he needed to tell Caroline. Sooner rather than later.

C aroline yawned as they walked back to their house. "I'm so glad I didn't have to finish cleaning the kitchen."

Marsh had taken the boys back to the house as soon as they'd finished dinner and put them to bed. She'd told Marsh he didn't need to come back to collect her, but she was glad he had.

"You'd done most of it," Marsh said.

"Cam said breakfast is at six."

"You're tired."

"Not too tired," Caroline said quickly, slanting a glance at her husband. She craved his touch and a peck on the cheek would not do. Once they made love again, it would feel as if their marriage was heading in the right direction.

Marsh drew her close. "I'm glad."

"It's so quiet here. Look at the stars. I don't think I've seen so many stars in all my life. I'd heard this is a good place to star watch, but I didn't realize the stars would fill the sky. They're so pretty."

"It's the perfect place for romance," Marsh said, and he stopped walking and swung her into his arms. His mouth covered hers seconds later, a kiss of promise, a kiss of hope, a kiss of passion.

Her body responded at once, softening against his. "I want you so much."

"We have a comfortable bed, one that's ready to climb into since you were so organized."

"Forethought and hope," she countered, her pulse jumping at the rough huskiness of his voice. He'd always made her feel this way. Eager for the physical, from the first time she'd seen him, she'd wanted his body, his touch. That had never changed even though things had gone wrong between them.

"Caroline, I love you and the boys. Never doubt that." He set her on her feet, caressed her cheek, then dropped his hand to cup her shoulder. "I know we haven't made love for a long time, but I want you very much. I didn't think I should rush you, that talking and working on our problems were more important than the physical side of our marriage. My idea was to woo you."

Caroline snorted and gave an embarrassed laugh. "For you, Marsh, I'm easy. I thought you didn't want me any longer. Your mother—"

Marsh opened the door to their house and led her inside. "I refuse to discuss my mother."

"Just this once," Caroline said, determined. "Your mother kept telling me I'd let myself go and that no man would want me. You were always so busy and you stopped sleeping in our bed. I didn't know...I thought that she was right." Caroline swallowed, finding this admission hard, even in the darkness of the house.

"I have never looked at another woman," Marsh said. "Not from the moment I first saw you. Mum doesn't know what she's talking about and I forbid you to listen to another word she says. If you have doubts, you come and ask me."

"You forbid?" Her lips quirked in the beginnings of a smile. Luckily he'd miss her amusement in this light.

"Most definitely," Marsh said. "No more talking. We're moving into the action phase."

Without warning, he lifted her off the floor again.

"Marsh," she protested. "I'm too heavy for you to tote around."

"Am I struggling," he countered.

"N-no." The truth. His breathing hadn't changed as he strode down the passage. How could he see in this inky blackness? He'd always been this way, and it seemed the boys had inherited his incredible eyesight.

Marsh dropped her on their bed. Unlike their bed in Middlemarch, she bounced instead of slipping into the dip made by long use.

Before she could blink, Marsh caged her between his body and the mattress. She breathed in his familiar scent and the flutters that had started earlier multiplied in intensity.

He kissed her. Slow and easy and the touch reverberated the length of her body. She reached for him, wanting to touch and explore in return.

"No," he whispered against her neck. "I won't last long if you touch me. Does your dress unzip at the back?"

"Yes." Bravery came easier in the darkness. Despite his assurances, her extra curves made her self-conscious.

"Turn over for me." Competent hands dealt with the zipper and whisked it open. Before she knew it, he had her out of her dress. A quick flick had her bra gaping and her matching panties—her last set of matching lingerie—drawn down her legs and tossed aside.

Marsh moved over her again. "Love your red hair, your sexy curves, Caroline." His voice emerged thick with emotion as if he meant the sentiment.

"You can't see me in the dark."

His chuckle prodded longing to life. "I can see enough." He kissed her again, his work-rough hands sliding over her shoulders, her arms and across her stomach. They never settled and did a good job of stirring her nerve endings until she vibrated like a cell phone.

He shaped her mouth with his tongue, then slid it inside, taking the kiss deeper. Her heart beat a little faster, and she grasped his shoulders, desperate for the pleasure hovering in the background. His cock sliding into her heat.

"When are you taking off your clothes?"

"About the time you're desperate and I've made you come once," he whispered, his breath warm against her neck. His breathing was as hard as hers. "I'm not lying about my lasting ability. Once I get inside you, I'll have the control of a green boy."

"We need to do this more often."

Marsh kissed her neck, giving her a hint of teeth this time, and she shuddered. Instantly, he stopped. "Did I hurt you?"

"No, don't stop. Please."

"No chance of that."

"Don't jinx us," she said. "We have two sons."

"Point taken." Marsh nipped her neck again, and a groan squeezed past her lips. His big hands shaped her breasts, his

111

knowledge of her body driving her to climax. She quivered, her heart knocking against her ribs as he moved down her body and splayed her legs. A wash of night air hit the juncture of her thighs, cool meeting warm.

"Marsh." His name held pleading, and she didn't care. She was more than ready to beg since she'd missed this closeness.

"Are you still on contraception?"

Caroline froze. "Why?"

"Kitten, I'd love to have another child with you, but right now, I want to concentrate on us and our boys. If we have another child, I want to know we're solid, and it would be nice to have one planned child. As much as I love our sons, both of them came as a surprise."

She dissected his words, prodded them for hidden meaning.

"Caroline?"

She sighed. "You're right. I am on the Pill, but in the flurry of packing I forgot to pick up my repeat script."

"We'll grab condoms next time we go to Tekapo or Twizel," Marsh said. "Or you can visit a doctor in Twizel. You'll want to register the boys, anyway."

"They're never sick. Honestly, they never catch the bugs at school. And I'd better not jinx that either. You're right," she conceded. "We're good for right now."

"Great." His lips grazed the side of one breast. "Now where were we?"

"Starting to get serious."

Marsh chuckled and teased her nipple, tugging it with his fingers while he kissed her other breast.

The tension that had claimed her faded, and she allowed herself to drift, clinging to Marsh and loving the heat emanating from his body. She couldn't wait to feel his hard muscles sliding against her body. His clothes were in the way.

Marsh slid a trail of kisses lower, licked over her hipbone. Funny, she'd forgotten how rough his tongue was—abrasive and stimulating. Her breath caught as she waited for his next move. She didn't have to wait long.

With his fingers beneath her naked butt, he lifted her toward his mouth, and that rough tongue of his dragged the length of her slit.

She swallowed, every part of her waiting, waiting, waiting for the hovering climax to explode. Thankfully, he didn't tease her but stroked firmly, giving extra attention to her clit. Enjoyment grew, pleasure flying up, up, up until one delicate wriggle of his tongue had her exploding, her empty channel pulsing, clutching at nothing.

"Marsh," she wailed.

"I've missed this so much," he muttered.

He stood, and she mourned the loss of his heat. She heard the rasp of his zipper, the whoosh as his shirt hit the floor. He returned to the bed, kissing her roughly, and she could taste herself.

"I want to fuck you so bad," Marsh said. "I've been dreaming of this night ever since we decided to come to the Mackenzie."

113

"We could have made love earlier."

"We could have, but I wanted to woo you."

She reached up and yanked both his ears. "I thought you didn't want me."

"Ouch, woman. I thought I proved to you when we almost made love that I wanted you. Every time I think of you my dick goes hard." He kissed her again, his tongue surging against hers. "Touch me."

"Where?"

"Everywhere. Anywhere. Need your hands on me. God, you drive me crazy, kitten. It's always been you. Only you." He cupped her breasts while still kissing her, his weight pushing her into the mattress. Then, he pulled away. "Let me take you from behind, kitten. I want to touch your breasts and have easy access to your clit while I drive into your pussy."

He'd always told her what he wanted to do to her, his constant talking making her so hot and desperate.

"Anything you want," she whispered. "I want you inside me."

He helped her into position—on her hands and knees. A sharp pain on one buttock had her starting and looking over her shoulder. "Did you bite my butt?"

"Yes. I like your backside, almost as much as the front."

That was another thing about Marsh. When they made love he left marks all over her. It never hurt at the time, but she ended up bruised and tingling. Well-loved too.

"You ready for me to fuck you?" His voice sounded deeper, hoarse.

"Bring it."

She heard his bark of laughter, then his cock nudged her entrance. He pushed into her with one easy thrust, his shaft going deep. She gasped, and he stilled.

"Okay."

"Yes."

"Thank god," she thought she heard him say, but then his busy hands distracted her, as did the surge and retreat of his cock. He upped the pace, one hand holding her in place while the other stroked her clit. His warm breath feathered across the base of her neck. She moaned, the combination of his touch and his cock doing it for her. Tingles of excitement fluttered to life, and she whimpered, this going much quicker than she'd expected. Her channel flexed around his cock and Marsh bit the fleshy pad at the base of her neck. Pain speared her, then the pleasure counteracted it.

Marsh gave a guttural groan, and his tongue flickered over the spot where he'd bitten her His hips moved in a frenzy, then he stilled, embedded in her flesh. Minute contractions told her he'd orgasmed. His tongue licked the same spot on her neck over and over, and each lash of his tongue made her vagina tighten around his shaft, a tiny drill of pleasure thrilling her.

Marsh lifted his head and pulled from her body. He turned her over and drew her into his arms, his fingers stroking that same spot. "I love you, kitten. I always have and I always will. Never forget that. Never," he added fiercely.

Fatigue settled in as he held her. "Love you too," she whispered, and that was the last thing she remembered before she fell asleep.

He'd marked her, bitten her in the feline manner, connected them as mates. Marsh stroked the tiny ridge of flesh and turned his head a fraction to study the site. It no longer bled since the enzymes in his saliva would speed healing. Regret, no, guilt surfaced. He should have told her before he marked her, claimed her as his, yet pride and satisfaction also coursed through his veins. He'd lacked control. Not only had he fucked her good and hard, tired her out, he'd lost control of his feline for a while there. Sharp claws had formed beneath his fingernails, forcing their way into prominence. Canines had made his speech deeper and the only thoughts pounding through his mind had been to take her.

Possess her.

Own her.

Mark her.

While the human part of him hadn't wanted her to fall pregnant, his feline had screamed in his mind, wanting another tie of belonging, so she could never leave them.

Hell. His breath whooshed out, and he dragged his free hand over his face. A disaster, yet a slow grin spread across his face, and he reveled in the pull of muscles. While he'd let his feline take control, he felt fantastic, as if a part of him had slotted into place. A missing part.

For the first time in his life, he truly belonged.

M arsh woke early. It was still dark outside and Caroline cuddled against his side. A sound. A growl? He rolled away from his mate and...his mate. A smile curved his lips even as he stood. A quick glance at Caroline showed she hadn't woken, and Marsh went to check on his sons. Ricky lay curled in a tight ball, only his head visible above the covers. He moved on to check on James, almost at his oldest son's bedroom when he heard another growl. What the hell?

He burst into the room. The growls were coming from James. His slight body twitched while his limbs jerked as if he were running in feline form.

"Steady there, James. It's all right," Marsh murmured, wondering what this meant. He and his friends hadn't experienced anything like this until the months before they shifted for the first time. Time to speak to Saber or Cam. And Caroline. She needed to learn the possible outcome of the boys' dreams.

James seemed to quieten and Marsh covered him and returned to bed.

"What is it? What's wrong?" Caroline murmured, her voice thick with sleep.

SHELLEY MUNRO

"James was having a bad dream. He's settled again and is fast asleep."

"Is it almost time for me to get up?"

"It's five thirty."

"Oh, man." Caroline sighed. "I need strong coffee to kick start me today."

Marsh reclined beside her, and unable to resist, pulled her against his body. "We could always make love again."

She yawned and kissed his neck, right on the marking site. "We could," she murmured, unaware of the havoc she'd created with her innocent touch.

His cock went rock-hard, his blood rushed south, leaving him dizzy.

Before the thought formed, he was kissing her, dragging their bodies even closer together, so she was in no doubt of his desire. His fingers strummed across her mark, and he gloried in the groan she made.

"I don't know what it is but that spot always makes me hot."

"Good to know," he purred.

He parted her legs and slipped into her heat, going slowly so he didn't hurt her. He needn't have worried because she groaned again and wrapped her legs around his hips, encouraging him without words.

"Yes," she muttered two thrusts later. "Yes, just like that."

Marsh grinned and did what she required. He'd missed this side of her, the demanding, knowing what she wanted in bed. If there was something she wanted, she'd never acted shy about asking him to act on her needs. Her channel contracted, and he saw stars, the purr of his feline rasping through his mind. Happy times all around. He kissed the side of her neck, his mouth searching for and finding the mark. It had healed already, leaving a raised scar. Instinct had him licking back and forth. Caroline gasped, her enjoyment of his ministrations making loud purrs rumble in his throat.

The muscles of her inner thighs quivered against him, her hips jerking with each of his hard thrusts. The tight, grasping heat of her pussy had his balls tightening, but it was her sexy little whimper that did him in. He exploded, unraveling within her embrace.

"Kitten," he groaned, his hips moving lazily now.

"My turn now." She wound her arms around his neck and laid her lips against his.

Humor leaped to life and his lips tilted up at the corners as he gave attention to her mark. A sneaky advantage he now had since the tales he'd heard regarding a feline mark seemed to be true. Each of his touches drove her wild. Her bright blue eyes fluttered closed as he fingered the spot. Her strawberry-blonde hair lay around her head in a snarl of curls. Uncharitable people called her hair *red*, usually in a disparaging tone. The color of her hair, combined with her blue eyes, had been one thing that had first attracted his attention. She was stunning. Curvy, and all his.

Now he had to confess about felines and what the mark meant.

He used his mouth on the spot, giving her a hint of teeth. Her fingernails dug into his shoulders, her hips moving restlessly. He slipped one hand between their bodies and sought her clit. Swollen and slippery, he caressed it with light but constant pressure. She hummed, her pussy flexing around his softening cock. He pushed on the mark with his free hand and caught her cry of pleasure with his mouth. Seconds later, she was coming, a flush on her cheeks. God, she was beautiful. He was a lucky man.

Her eyes flicked open, and she smiled. "That was amazing. Not a bad way to start the day."

"I second that." He sighed, sated with pleasure and loath to leave this cocoon of togetherness.

The alarm pipped a warning—the weird noise it made before it went full throttle into wake-up mode. Marsh reached over and slapped it off.

Caroline sighed. "Guess I'd better get going."

"I'll check on the boys while you grab a quick shower."

"Thanks." She peered out the window. "It's so dark out there. No wonder Cam recommended I take Maria's torch."

"If the dark worries you, I can go up with you. The boys should be all right for a few minutes."

"Don't be silly. I'll be fine. It's not as if I have to worry about getting mugged."

Marsh kissed her cheek. "Okay. I'll wait until the boys wake and get them breakfast."

"School is in session this morning. Jan, the woman in charge of schooling, said both boys can go."

"I'll deliver them to school and then go out with some of the boys to get a handle on my workday. Is that okay?"

"Perfect. Can you tell Jan I'll be working up at the main house? Tell her I'll come to collect the boys after I serve lunch."

"Will do."

Caroline rolled out of bed. "Ow, ow, ow."

"What's wrong?"

"Sore muscles. Nothing a hot shower won't fix."

Happiness caught his breath. "Any reason for sore muscles?"

Caroline huffed. "You know why I have sore muscles, mister." She fumbled for the switch near the door and flicked it on, flooding the bedroom with bright light.

Amusement flooded him now, as she blinked at him like a morepork, New Zealand's native owl. "Would you forgive me if I offered to give you a massage once the boys go to bed tonight?"

"Deal." She winked at him and sashayed from the bedroom, naked and sexy.

His mate.

His grin stretched so wide his mouth hurt.

Chapter 7

Kitchen Duties

C aroline let herself out the front door and exhaled as the frigid morning air slapped her. Gloves. She'd need to find her gloves, scarf and warm hat. She closed the door with a click and marched to the end of their short driveway. The darkness was absolute as was the silence. She took a moment to switch on the torch, a comforting circle of light piercing the inky-black and illuminating her way.

The hair at the back of her neck prickled without warning, and she froze mid-step. She glanced over her shoulder, seeing nothing even though her night vision had kicked in and she could see faint outlines of neighboring houses and farm buildings.

"Silly," she muttered. "There is nothing out here."

She forced herself to move again, her steps noisy on the gravel underfoot. Heck, she'd told Marsh she'd be fine. Now she wished she'd accepted his offer. She increased her pace until she was running, certain someone lurked in the shadows, watching her progress to the main house. A thin coating of perspiration moistened her brow. She slowed to wipe her sweaty palms on her jeans.

"You have an overactive imagination," she whispered, to keep herself from crossing the remaining distance at a sprint. She forced herself to halt and turned a slow circle, casting her senses out to gather information. Nothing. She wished for the bat ears and eagle sight of Marsh and their boys.

An uneasy laugh escaped, and she resumed walking, fiercely glad when her hand closed around the door handle of the outer entrance to the main house kitchen.

Once she flicked on the light, the familiar surroundings of the kitchen calmed her galloping nerves. Shaking her head at her silliness, Caroline peeled off her coat, hung it on a coat hook near the door, washed her hands and got to work. Three batches of blueberry muffins and two loaves of fruit bread later, she admitted that the extreme darkness and the new surroundings had messed with her head. Stupid city girl, she thought as she set the table for breakfast. You'd think the years of living in Middlemarch would prepare her for the high country of the Mackenzie.

The outer door opened, and two of the employees entered, masculine laughter filling the air. Several men followed and the dining area of the large kitchen was soon awash with cheerful, hungry men.

"Something smells good," one of the men said. He winked at her, his gaze a brilliant green. "I worried when someone said Maria wasn't cooking. Dinner last night was tasty, and I can't wait to see what you've made us today."

"I can smell bacon," an older man said as he whisked off his knitted beanie and hung it on the back of a wooden chair.

"Sausages. Eggs," a tall and thin man, not long out of his teenage years added.

"Start with cereal," Caroline ordered. "I'll have something hot for you in ten minutes."

Breakfast passed in a rush and flurry. She fed ten men and sent them on their way with packed lunches since Cam had told her the previous night the men would be out the entire day.

Cam appeared looking rumpled and worried.

"How is Maria?"

"Not so good. She's complaining of nausea and pain in her lower abdominal. She has a fever."

"Did she keep down the soup?"

"No. I'm going to fly her to Timaru," Cam said.

"Anything you need me to do?"

"Just keep the men fed. They know what to do on the station."

Cam rushed off and Caroline went back to her kitchen duties.

The morning seemed too short. Having no idea of what Maria had planned for meals, Caroline checked the pantry plus the walk-in freezer, and after assessing the ingredients, she planned menus for the next week.

"Mum! Mum!" A mother opened the door, and Ricky barreled inside, his face alive with excitement. "We played, and we drawed pictures and had a story."

James arrived at a more sedate pace, a carry bag in his right hand and his attention on a girl his age.

"Hi, Caroline. I'm not sure if you got everyone's names straight yesterday. I'm Dara. Jan asked me to deliver your sons since with Cam in Timaru, they were short a man. Your man got himself recruited to help with the dipping."

"Thanks," Caroline said.

"Looks as if you're recruited too."

"I don't mind. I prefer to keep busy."

"Why don't I take your boys for you for the afternoon?"

"No, I couldn't—"

"It's no problem. James and my daughter are already firm friends. Chelsea loves to draw and I hear James does too. And your little one is yawning so much, I figure he'll sleep part of the afternoon."

"Are you sure? I'd like to get a head start on the cooking. I don't want to dig into Maria's stock of frozen meals too much."

"I'm sure." She flapped a hand in unconcern. "We take turns with the kids, so we can get alone time. It's a team effort if you live here on Glenshee."

"I'm discovering that," Caroline said. "James." She squatted beside her son, trying to hide the wince from her protesting muscles. "You be good for Dara." She tapped his nose. "Okay?"

James nodded. "We're going for a walk to draw the mountains."

Amused, she stood. "Sounds as if everyone is happy with this deal. Thanks, I appreciate it."

"No prob. See you later." Dara herded the children out of the kitchen. "I'll deliver them back at dinner time."

Caroline started the pies and with those in the oven, she moved on to chopping vegetables for a pot of soup.

The phone rang, and she wiped her hands on a nearby hand towel. "Hello?"

"It's Cam. Maria has appendicitis. She's in the operating room now. The doctors said if we'd left it any longer it might have ruptured."

"But she will be okay?"

"Yes, I think so."

"Book into a motel so you get a decent sleep," Caroline said.

"I might do that, once I know Maria is in recovery. I appreciate you taking over the kitchen. It wasn't the original plan."

"It's no problem." The truth. For once, Caroline felt as if she was doing something useful, instead of being James and Ricky's mother. Not that she didn't love her two sons, but sometimes in Middlemarch her identity got buried.

Dara delivered the boys back at five. Caroline settled them in the kitchen with an early dinner since they were both drooping with tiredness.

"Did you have a good time?" she asked.

"We drew pictures, and we played soccer," James said. "It's fun playing here."

Caroline nodded. "Ricky, did you have fun?"

"We played tag, and we ran and ran and ran." He puffed out his chest. "I like running."

Caroline smoothed his hair. "That's good."

The men started arriving for dinner just after six, their hair wet and slicked back after their quick showers. They'd changed into clean clothes and brought their appetites.

"Hey, kitten." Marsh slipped his arm around her waist and hauled her close for a kiss, even with their audience.

"Hey," someone shouted. "Don't molest the cook. We might miss out on dinner, and it sure smells good."

Marsh gave her another quick kiss and released her to greet their sons. "I have an in with this cook," he tossed over his shoulder to his new workmates. "She'll feed me, but you lot will need to mind your manners."

Several of the men hooted, making Caroline laugh. A small part of her had worried how they'd fit in because they couldn't leave the station if it didn't work for them. This was their last chance, but now after only a day, she felt at home. The boys were happy, and she slid a glance at Marsh. He was joking with several of the men, and she hadn't seen him look this content for a long time. She bustled around the kitchen and moved the boys, so she could set the table for the men.

This change had been good for the entire family.

127

"Why don't you put the kids in the lounge in front of the TV?" one of the older men suggested. "They can go to sleep on the couch. Cam and Maria won't mind."

"Thanks," Marsh said. "I'll take them to the house once we've had dinner."

Caroline served soup and produced a steak and kidney pie and platters of vegetables for their main course.

"Caroline, you need to eat too. You don't need to run after us," one of the men said.

They chorused an agreement, so she sat and ate a bowl of soup and a slice of fresh bread.

Marsh took her hand under the table, the physical contact thrilling her.

"I want to get a head start on tomorrow, so I don't have to work as hard," Caroline said.

"I can stay."

Caroline searched his expression and softened inside. He was a good man. Nothing like his parents. A miracle, which made her curious about his older brother and how things had been before his death. "Take the boys home once you've eaten. They'll sleep better in their own beds. I'll be an hour tops."

"I still owe you a massage," Marsh said.

"One hour," she promised.

Once Marsh left, she had the kitchen to herself. The men had loaded their dishes into the dishwasher and there wasn't much left to clean up. She put on the crockpot and prepared a steak and vegetable stew. With that underway, she made a batch of cookie dough—one she could freeze and take out as needed. The more items she could add to the freezer, the easier it would be in the future.

An hour and a half later, she switched off the kitchen lights and made her way home. The moon hung low on the inky-black horizon but the stars filled the sky, so many twinkly lights it was difficult to know where to look. Beautiful. She stopped and did a slow twirl, appreciating the enormity of the sight and how most people never got the chance to see this natural beauty.

With a happy sigh, she began walking, knowing Marsh was waiting for her. She could see their house, the porch light burning like a welcoming beacon.

A torch bounced in her pocket with each step, but the dark didn't seem so forbidding this evening. This morning—well, she felt embarrassed of her girlish behavior and was glad no one had witnessed her city-girl panic.

No sooner had she finished this thought than a growl came from her right. She froze, her pulse jumping into flight-mode. She strained to listen, but silence greeted her, the only audible sound her own choppy breathing.

"You're being silly." Caroline forced her legs to move again, walking faster, faster. She flew across the gravel road and darted into their driveway. Her sweaty hands grasped the door handle, and it turned. As she opened the door, she glanced over her shoulder and swore she saw a big black cat staring at her. She blinked and when she focused again, it had disappeared. Either that or her mind was playing tricks on her.

James had drawn black cats this afternoon, and Ricky had run around madly doing cat growls. Her imagination had taken the obvious road and was now having a joke at her expense.

"Caroline. You're home." Marsh prowled toward her, stalking like a cat, his smile toothy. Were those...no! God, this physical work had tired her. She blinked several times, and everything in her world righted when she looked at her husband again.

"I enjoyed today, but I'm not used to the physical work. The pots and cooking trays are huge."

Concern shone in Marsh's eyes. "If it's too much for you, you need to say. One of the other wives will come and help."

"No, it's fine. I enjoyed myself. The last few years—I haven't felt useful. Whenever I cooked for the shearers on your parents' farm, your mother made out it was her who did the hard work."

"I wish you'd told me," Marsh said. "She had no right to treat you that way."

"Forget it. I didn't want to worry you." And she was ashamed of folding so easily. She should have stood up to Marsh's mother.

"This move is good for both of us. I enjoyed working with the men today. They're a close-knit group yet they were very welcoming. Felix said I'd appreciate Glenshee's benefits."

"That's great, because the boys are happy too, and I loved my day, even though it was busy."

"Come and sit with me. I'll make you a cup of your milo and run you a bath."

"Sounds like heaven."

Marsh coddled her, and ten minutes later he started on the promised massage. The scent of lavender oil filled the air, and she lay on her stomach on top of their bed. His hands glided over her shoulders and back, digging into sore muscles and loosening kinks.

She moaned at the sheer decadent pleasure of it, and his chuckle filled the air.

"Not too loud. You'll wake the boys."

"Don't think so," she retorted. "I checked on them while you were running the bath. They were both sound asleep."

"Well, in that case." He turned her over, and his expression had her licking her lips.

"Oh."

"Oh, indeed." With great deliberation, he unfastened the buttons of the shirt he'd worn for dinner. He tugged it off his broad shoulders and set it on a chair. His jeans were next.

"No underwear," she murmured, her avid gaze enjoying the scenery.

"I've missed this playful side of you."

"I've missed us."

"Me too," he whispered, and then he kissed her, hands scented by lavender oil caressing her shoulders, her neck, cupping her breasts.

She sighed against his mouth, wrapping her hands around his shoulders. Already, aroused from his touches during the massage, she writhed against him, desiring a deeper contact.

"Now," she gasped. "Please."

He guided his cock to her and pushed inside in slow increments. This loving...it felt new and special, so special.

"I love you, Marsh."

"A man never tires of hearing his sexy wife say that."

A week ago she'd have second-guessed his words, but the change in scenery, a new confidence left her doubts lingering in the dust.

He thrust at speed, driving them both higher, then nibbled on a spot at the base of her neck. He'd bitten her there the previous night. It had hurt, then the pleasure of her orgasm had swamped her and she'd forgotten the brief pain. This morning she'd expected a bloody mess, but there was only a raised mark. When she'd fingered it while in the shower, sparks of enjoyment had coalesced in her pussy. Weird, but every time Marsh touched that spot she lit up like a vibrant firework.

This time was no exception. She gasped and tumbled into intense bliss. The sex between them had always been good, but last night and now—exceptional.

Marsh shuddered above her, his head thrown back, his pretty green eyes shrouded as he climaxed. His face always looked so fierce and primal during their lovemaking. Lucky, she knew and trusted him because that face could scare a woman.

She stared at him, watched for his expression to soften and his eyes to open. There. Intense love for her blazed from him, and she smiled in return.

Lazily, they rearranged their bodies and Marsh snapped off the lamp on his side of the bed. She snuggled into his warmth and thought she'd never been this happy.

Caroline woke the next morning, a few minutes before the alarm was due to chime. She reached over to slap the off button.

"You're awake," Marsh whispered next to her ear.

"Yes. I should get moving. I didn't think to organize the boys."

"All in hand." Marsh sounded smug. "Dara said it was no trouble collecting them after the school session. I'll drop them off at school before I head off to join the men. Hamish said it won't matter if I'm late. They know we're juggling family commitments."

"Are you sure?"

He moved back a fraction and slid his hand over her butt. He gave it a quick slap. "You'd better get moving or you'll have a kitchen load of hungry men and no food prepared."

Caroline rolled out of bed. "Thanks." She leaned over to give him a kiss and laughed when she noticed him leering at her breasts. She tweaked his nose. "Enough of that, Mr. Rutherford. We don't have time for mischief this morning."

"Is that what you call it?"

With another laugh, she scuttled off to shower and change. Fifteen minutes later, after checking on the boys, she left the house, her steps brisk, her gaze darting from left to right as she hurried to the main homestead.

She arrived to find Hamish, the man the workers took orders from while Cam was away, sitting at the dining table, a mug of tea in his hands. The stew she'd put on to cook in the crockpot smelled amazing.

"Am I late?"

"No, you're not late, lass. There was a problem with the stock late last night. We're missing a hundred head of our prize merinos."

"Rustlers?"

"Looks like."

"Rustlers hit around Middlemarch just before we left. Marsh's father lost stock, and no one saw a thing. Evidently, they are brazen thieves."

"So were this lot. It was pure chance I was outside and heard a truck."

"What time was this?"

"About nine."

"Something growled at me while I was walking home." A nervous laugh escaped. "Scared the crap out of me. Do you think they had dogs?"

He shot her a sharp look. "Possibly. Anyhow, we'll be more alert now. Damn if Cam doesn't have enough to worry him."

Caroline checked on the stew in the crockpot. Perfect.

"Smells good," Hamish said.

"Breakfast will be half an hour yet. If you can keep a secret, I'll give you a plate now. That's if you're okay eating meat at this time of the day."

"Sounds good," he said in his gruff voice. "It's good of you to help out. It's one thing off Cam's mind."

"I enjoy cooking, and you're full of compliments. It's making me feel important."

"Food is important, lass. We can't work on empty stomachs."

"No chance of that," she said as she lifted the lid off the enormous slow cooker.

Caroline gave Hamish his stew and chatted to him about life on Glenshee station.

"Gets cold in the middle of winter. Didn't have a big storm last year. Reckon we're due."

"I've always lived in the south," Caroline said. "I know about bad winters."

"We'll get cut off," he warned.

"Are you trying to scare me?"

He barked out a laugh. "Maybe. You're a nice lady. I don't want you to go silly with cabin fever."

"I'll be fine."

The phone rang, and Hamish rose to answer the call. Cam, she deduced as she cracked three dozen eggs and whisked in milk and condiments. By the time the men tromped into the kitchen, some bleary-eyed, the eggs were ready and bacon and sausages kept warm in the oven.

"Can I have a volunteer to make toast?"

"I'll do it." Hamish grabbed the stack of bread she'd cut and shoved six pieces into the toaster while the men started on cereal. "Most of you have heard that someone has stolen our sheep. Since the bastards found it so easy the first time, they'll return. We will take turns doing night patrols. I'll let you know times once I've worked out the logistics. Cam and Maria will be back today since they're discharging Maria this morning." He glanced at Caroline. "He's trying to organize one of Maria's friends to take over part of the cooking, so we don't scare you off, Caroline."

She nodded, part of her disappointed but at least she'd have time to work on the dresses she'd promised Tomasine and Isabella.

"I want team one to muster the sheep at the top paddock. You'll need to stay over at Red Hill hut tonight. Team two you're on rabbit patrol this evening in the western paddock. I want you to check the fencing in the Hut paddock and do a count of the flock. I want to know the exact tally of missing sheep. Team three we're going to crutch the ewes and give them health checks." He plucked the slices of toast free and handed them off to the men before loading more bread in the toaster. "Any questions?"

Once again, the differences between the way Cam ran his farm and Marsh's father struck Caroline. The men here worked as a team with little grumbling and they attacked their working day in enthusiasm.

136

With their bellies full and tasks allocated, the men drifted from the kitchen, leaving her alone. Caroline got stuck into the dishes, then started to make more bread.

The *whop-whop* of the helicopter sounded overhead midmorning, and she washed her floury hands to put on the jug to make a hot drink. Cam and Maria entered the kitchen ten minutes later, and Caroline turned to greet them.

Maria's face was pale, her vibrant personality missing as she forced a smile. "Thanks for covering for me."

"No problem. You look as if you need to rest."

"I'm tired. Didn't sleep well with the ward hullabaloo."

"Hospitals are noisy places," Caroline said.

"I'm thinking of taking Maria for two weeks holiday. Her sister keeps asking us to visit her in the Bay of Islands, but there is never time. This health scare has made me realize too much work isn't good." Cam's voice was gruff, his expression concerned as he studied his wife. "We haven't had a holiday for years."

"You should go," Caroline said. "I'm coping with the meals. Hamish has stuff under control on the station." She crossed her fingers behind her back, not wanting to worry Cam with the stock thefts.

"What do you think, Maria? We could leave tomorrow."

"Caroline will need help in the kitchen. I haven't found anyone to help yet. She should have time off at the same time as Marsh."

"Hush, sweetheart. Let's get you up to bed and comfy, then I'll sort out logistics."

Chapter 8

Knife Lady

Three days later, Caroline settled James and Ricky at the kitchen table with paper and crayons. She gave her youngest son a stern glance. "No drawing on the table. If I see one little drawing not on your paper, I won't give you any cake or cookies for ten days. That's one day for every finger," she added when he opened his mouth. "Do you understand?"

He nodded vigorously, dark curls falling over his eyes. She hadn't considered haircuts. Someone on the station must cut hair or maybe somewhere in Twizel. Marsh had promised them a trip to see Mount Cook this coming weekend.

A weekend. She was trying not to get too excited, but it was such a treat to go somewhere as a family.

"Should I make Shepherd's Pie or do a roast dinner tonight?"

"Roast," James said.

She ruffled his hair as he looked up from his drawing. Another leopard. "Do you like leopards?"

He nodded, his black curls as long as his brother's.

"They come with spots too."

He cocked his head and considered his picture. Two large leopards lounged on rocks while two smaller leopards played below. All leopards were soot black while the background in his drawing resembled the station scenery. As she watched, James sketched a figure—a woman. "Why is there a lady in your picture?"

James glanced up at her and shrugged. "Just is."

She smoothed a rebellious curl. "I think you will look after us in our old age with the proceeds from your wonderful drawings." He'd drawn a lady in his other big cat drawings too even though she'd told him that his big cats might eat the lady.

Satisfied the boys were occupied, she turned her mind to the coming meals. The packed lunches were ready for the men who were working away from the homestead today, and someone would collect them soon. Six of the men were coming for lunch and she'd have the full contingent for dinner because the mustering team had arrived back from the far hut. Vegetables. She could do them now and parboil them.

Caroline got to work on potatoes, pumpkin and kumara, peeling the vegetables, washing and tossing them in one of Maria's huge pots.

A scratching noise at the outer door had her head lifting. An instant later the door sprang open and something big, something black, burst inside. Caroline let out an *eep* of surprise then screamed as she realized a humongous leopard had entered her kitchen. She grabbed the kitchen knife.

"Don't move," she ordered the boys, her voice holding a distinct tremor.

The black leopard skidded to a stop and stared at her with intense green eyes.

Caroline stayed rooted in place, knife held in front of her as she stared back. "Shoo! Get out of my kitchen." She waved the knife, glanced at her two boys. Thankfully, they weren't doing anything to attract the animal's attention.

The leopard prowled closer.

"Out!" Caroline screeched. Her heart tried to claw its way up her throat. "Get out!"

Outside, she heard running feet. Marsh appeared in the doorway.

"What's wrong? I've come to—" He spotted the leopard. "Crap."

Caroline expected him to run for help, to pick up the nearest weapon, to protect the boys. He did none of these things.

"Out," he ordered, standing aside.

To Caroline's astonishment, the leopard obeyed Marsh and trotted out the door.

"I've come for the lunches."

"Where did it come from? What's it doing here? Why is it wandering around?"

Marsh entered the kitchen and closed the door behind him. He crossed the distance between them and pried the knife from her hand. She dropped it on the counter with a clatter. Reaction set in and she trembled.

Marsh drew her into his arms. "Shhh, it's all right."

"B-but there was a leopard in the kitchen." She glanced at the boys and neither of them appeared upset. "A black one, just like James's drawings."

"I know. Caroline." Marsh cursed, and she pulled back in surprise. He seldom swore, and she hadn't heard him curse since they'd arrived at Glenshee. "I have to tell you something."

"What?"

"Damn, I need to get back with the lunches. They're waiting on me."

"You can't go outside with that leopard." She gripped his forearm. "We have to let the others know. The children... What are you doing?"

Marsh flung off his shirt and bent to unfasten his work boots. "This is the quickest way."

Caroline stared in bemusement as Marsh stripped off every item of clothing.

"Stand over there with the boys. I don't want you near the knife."

When she hesitated in confusion, he shunted her in their sons' direction.

"But the leopard—"

"I'm getting to that. Damn, I'm an idiot."

Caroline opened her mouth to ask questions, then blinked. What was wrong with Marsh? His face, his arms... She blinked again. Hard.

Marsh's body shimmered and glowed. His big shoulders bowed, and he hunched farther forward, dropping to his hands and knees.

Marsh, he...she closed her eyes and opened them again just in time to see Marsh's handsome face turn into something different. Something feline. Black.

The transformation didn't take long, but time ticked off in slow motion.

Her legs trembled so badly, she grasped for the nearest chair and directed her body toward the hard wooden seat. She missed and fell.

The big black leopard—Marsh—prowled toward her and she scrambled backward in a panic before the wall at her back halted retreat.

"Stay there. Don't come any closer."

The leopard let out a huff and sat on his haunches.

Ricky wriggled off his chair and raced toward the leopard.

Caroline opened her mouth but only a croak emerged.

Ricky threw himself at the leopard and crawled on its back.

"Ricky, come here," she managed.

"I want to play," Ricky said.

The leopard—she couldn't think of it as her husband—nudged Ricky with his big head and directed him back to his seat. Then, he stood back, and the reverse happened.

The feline face wavered, bones creaked and cracked as they reshaped to the more familiar figure of her husband. Without looking at her, he grabbed his clothes and dressed.

He glanced at her, his face a map of disappointment. "I should have told you years ago, when we first married, but Mum and Dad didn't approve of me marrying a human and they thought you'd freak and tell everyone. Saber told me to tell you as soon as possible. Hell, Cam told me too." He dragged a hand through his hair. "I wanted our marriage on a stable path again before I told you. I intended to tell you this weekend."

"Saber told you?"

"The Mitchell family are the same as me."

"All of them?" she whispered, her mind trying and failing to reconcile the information with her knowledge of the Mitchell family.

"Not Emily. She's human." He glanced at the counter where she'd set out the lunches ready for collection. Two red chiller-bags.

Her mind refused to slip into gear. "Cam?"

"Everyone here apart from Maria."

Shock kicked like an ornery mule, collecting her in the middle of the chest until it felt as if her breathing came through a straw.

A knock came on the door. It opened and Dara stuck in her head. "I've come to take the boys to school. Sorry, I'm late today."

Caroline flinched. "James? Ricky?"

"They will take after me," Marsh said, his gaze steady on hers.

144

Dara entered the kitchen and glanced at Marsh.

"Take the boys to school," he instructed.

Caroline wanted to protest. She opened her mouth to protest and snapped it shut again. Her sons were happy. They'd been here almost a week and her sons had bloomed. They both loved school and playing with the other kids. Leopards...

A man stood aside as Dara shepherded out James and Ricky. Caroline heard their high-pitched greetings as they joined Dara's children.

Saul Sinclair entered the kitchen. "Sorry. I thought my aunt Maria would be in the kitchen."

"It's all right, Saul," Marsh said. "Didn't Cam ring you? Maria had appendicitis, and he took her up north to visit her sister."

"Hell. I've been away," Saul said. "Dad isn't speaking to me, so I didn't bother contacting home. Caroline, I'm so sorry I gave you a fright. Is Maria going to be okay?"

"She's fine," Marsh said.

Caroline gaped at Saul who she'd met in Middlemarch since his family had a farm not far from the Rutherfords. She scanned the concern in his green eyes, his tousled black hair. They looked the same. In the past, she'd noticed, wondered, but she'd let it pass. Most of the residents of Middlemarch were descended from Scottish settlers. She'd decided it was the Celtic gene making itself known.

Not Celtic.

Not human.

Feline.

"I've got to go," Marsh said. "Caroline, we'll talk this evening. You know where the car keys are. You can leave, but I hope our marriage means something to you."

"I can take the lunches and work in your place," Saul offered.

Marsh hesitated. "No." He glanced at Caroline. "Nothing has changed. I love you. I love our boys. Try to remember that." After another searching glance, he picked up the lunches and left her with Saul.

"I can take over in the kitchen. Maria taught me how to cook, and I always help her when I visit."

Caroline pushed to her feet and hugged herself, suddenly cold in the warm kitchen. Everyone living at Glenshee Station was a leopard. Everyone except Maria. She shuddered, her mind shying from the truth.

She'd never known, never suspected.

If anything, Marsh's frequent absences at odd hours of the night had sent her down Affair Lane. Shapeshifters...never in a million years would she have guessed.

"I'll make a cup of coffee or would you prefer tea?" Saul's brows rose as he waited.

"Coffee."

Saul burst into action, proving that he was telling the truth about working with Maria. He had a cup of coffee and a chocolate chip cookie ready in minutes.

"Thanks." She sat at the table and picked up the china mug, cradling it in her hands and letting the warmth seep into her frozen body. Her mind had gone numb. Shapeshifters. Her husband. Her sons. She had no idea what to do.

Saul took a seat at the table and munched on a cookie. "These are good. Did you make them?"

She nodded.

"I make excellent scones and pikelets."

She sipped her coffee and nodded again.

"You could talk to Emily."

"I'm making a macaroni bake with cheese, bacon and vegetables. I have minestrone soup and fresh bread plus sandwich fillings. Cookies and fruit to finish their lunch."

"Sounds good. Dinner?" Saul picked up the change of conversation without a blink.

"Roast beef, Yorkshire pudding. Roast vegetables and gravy. Lemon meringue pie for dessert."

"I'll help with the vegetables once we finish our coffee. I see you've started. If we do extras, we can use them for breakfast."

Caroline nodded and forced herself to still. She must resemble a nodding puppet. She finished her drink and stood, a part of her surprised her legs were holding her weight.

"Caroline." Saul's tone sounded sharp. "Are you okay?"

No, she wasn't okay. Her entire world had shifted on its axis, and she didn't know what to do, what to think, how she should react. She knew nothing.

Marsh had to force himself to stride from the homestead. He gripped the handles of the chiller-bags and willed his feline to settle. Caroline had acted terrified, horrified. *Freaked.*

He'd known it would be a shock, but he'd expected a calm discussion, not a wide-eyed, knife-wielding woman. And she didn't even know the worst of it yet. The other night he'd marked her, claiming her as his mate. Neither of them would do well apart.

Her body had accepted the mark, his enzymes mixing with hers to promote healing. She felt something when he caressed the spot.

She was his mate and, damn it, they'd get past this.

He refused to think of any alternative.

Chapter 9

Shock

S aul took control of the kitchen, and once Dara dropped the boys off from school, he shooed her out the door. In a daze, she directed the boys to the path winding past late-blooming roses, toward their home.

Her mind spun, going in endless circles of disbelief, unease. Shock. She thrust her hands in her pockets and seconds later, dragged them back out to fiddle with the strap of the bag containing the boys' toys.

"Can we explore? The lake is down that road. Can we show you?" James asked.

"There are fish," Ricky said.

"Sure. It's a nice day. We'll pack our afternoon tea and go for a walk." She didn't want to stay in the house. The fresh air might help her troubled thoughts. Why hadn't Marsh told her? His parents...they must have laughed behind her back. No wonder they'd always treated her as an outsider, because that was exactly what she was—a human amongst a community of leopard shapeshifters. God, it was the stuff of fairy tales. Nightmares.

"Mum." James tugged her sleeve.

"We're home."

She opened the door and pushed inside. "James, put your school stuff away and find a warm jacket to wear. I'll help Ricky."

She studied her eldest son. He didn't appear bothered by watching a leopard burst into the kitchen or seeing Marsh transform...shift...whatever they called the change from human to animal. His lack of concern pushed another thought to the front of her mind. "Have you seen leopards before? Is that why you draw them?"

"Yes," he whispered, his green gaze shooting to his feet.

"When? Why didn't you tell me?"

"I told Daddy. He said that they wouldn't hurt me and not to tell you in case it made you worry."

Anger pulsed in her then. He'd told James to lie.

James continued. "Daddy said he was gonna...going to tell you at the weekend. He said he'd 'plain everything."

"I see." She softened her crisp words with a smile. "It's okay. Find your jacket. Come on, Ricky. Let's hustle."

"Hustle!" Ricky shouted and sprinted along the passage.

Caroline supervised Ricky, then grabbed an orange straw basket from her wardrobe. In the kitchen, she packed biscuits and bottles of water plus three apples she'd picked off the tree in their back garden.

The phone went when they were on the point of leaving. She picked it up.

"Caroline?"

"Yes."

"It's Isabella. I wondered how you're getting on with my dress. The clothes you gave us to sell at the market before you left Middlemarch sold out in half an hour. It was a lucky day when you couldn't fit them into your car. People didn't even care that some of them were secondhand. I have a business proposition—"

"Are you a leopard?"

A startled silence met her question. She heard a soft intake of breath. "Did Marsh tell you?"

"One charged into the homestead kitchen this morning, and I grabbed a knife to defend myself."

"I see."

"Not me. I don't understand anything."

"It's simple," Isabella said. "You can walk away from Marsh, but he's the same man you loved enough to marry. He'd never hurt you. I know because stuff like that gets around the Middlemarch grapevine."

"But our children..."

"Are just like Marsh. You need to decide if you want to leave your sons—"

"They're my children too," Caroline snapped, incensed at the idea she'd walk away from her sons.

"Then, you've made your decision," Isabella pointed out. "You need to talk with Marsh, tell him your fears, but the truth is there are far more dangerous people and creatures in the world to fear than us. Consider that, Caroline. Two human men stalked Lisa Jordan not long after the Middlemarch ball. Someone wanted to kill Tomasine. What I'm trying to say is that bad things happen in all parts of our society. Different isn't a bad thing, but really, shifters aren't that different to you. Ask Emily. Ask Tomasine about the Middlemarch shifters. Ask Maria. We all want love. We want a safe place to live with our families. Think about that. I'll ring you again tomorrow. I still want to talk business. Remember, ring Emily if you need someone to confide in. Okay? She's the perfect person to talk to because she's been through this."

Caroline nodded, then realized Isabella couldn't see and gave verbal affirmation. "Thanks." Something Isabella said registered. "Wait, my stuff sold?"

"Yes." Isabella sounded smug. "I manned the stall since Emily was busy with the organizing part and answering questions. If you can make more clothes, I can sell them for you."

"Maria and Cam are away on holiday at present. I haven't even unpacked my sewing machine."

"Well, if you get the urge, go for it. Talk to you tomorrow." Isabella hung up.

Caroline stared at the phone for an instant before returning it to the charger. Isabella had given her the blunt truth, yet she felt better for having Marsh's words confirmed.

"Mum, are we going?" James asked.

"Yes."

"Where are you going?" a deep voice asked.

Caroline jumped, startled by her husband. They stared at each other for a long moment.

"To the lake," Ricky shouted.

"Sounds like fun," Marsh said without breaking their connection. "Can I come?"

Caroline nodded, finding the lump in her throat too big to push past a string of words. Thoughts and questions continued to whir through her head, but now wasn't the time. "Let me grab another drink and more cookies."

The lake glittered a brilliant blue in the sunshine and filled part of a valley. A craggy hill with its steep faces exposed to the elements glinted under the sun. Marsh and the boys led her to a small sandy beach and several other families were enjoying the autumn sunshine and mild weather while it lasted.

Marsh peeled off his coat and handed it to her. "You can sit on this. I'm going to shift. Some of the others were playing in feline form and they shifted back when they smelled your approach."

"I don't smell." Her chin jutted upward, and she glared at him.

He reached out to cup her face, but he halted the move and dropped his hand to his side. "We have better hearing than a

153

human and our sense of smell is good. If I shift, the others will know it's okay for them to play in cat form. They've been holding back for your sake."

Heck. She'd had no idea. "I'm sorry. I didn't know."

"It's all right. I intended to tell you this weekend."

"What about sight? Is that better?"

"That too."

She nodded and concentrated on spreading out Marsh's jacket. Feeling the weight of a stare, she glanced up and saw they were the center of attention. Rumors had spread about her freak-out.

"Can we swim?" James asked, pointing to his friends.

"We don't have togs or towels," Caroline said.

"They don't need them today. It's not far home, and we can put them in the shower as soon as we get back," Marsh said.

Caroline nodded since James and Ricky were casting envious gazes at their friends—all of whom were swimming naked. She could hardly deny them this. "Okay."

"I'll go in with them." He eyed their sons. "I'll go swimming with you, but no pulling my tail."

Ricky giggled as he came to her to get undressed.

A few minutes later, they ran to the lake with Marsh loping at their side. Several other adults shifted to their cat forms and trotted toward the water to join in the fun.

For the next hour, Caroline watched the children and several black leopards play. The older children played water polo while the younger children had splashing competitions and swimming lessons. The adults in leopard form supervised, taking expert care of every child who was taking part.

Isabella was right. The shapeshifters were like regular families. They cared for their children and each other. Although none of them had approached her at the lake, she couldn't blame them after her knife-wielding panic. Her job to make the first move.

Now that she was calmer, she could act and think with logic. They'd been at Glenshee Station for almost a week. Everyone she spoke with or fed in the homestead kitchen had treated her with care and respect. She'd seen the way Cam worried about Maria, witnessed the strength of their marriage.

If she and Marsh could have the same strong, loving partnership, she'd be a happy woman. Isabella was right. She'd talk with Marsh, ask questions.

Caroline sighed. She wished Marsh had told her sooner because she felt like such an idiot.

Marsh trotted over to her, herding their shrieking sons. He stopped to shake and Caroline clapped her hand over her mouth when Ricky copied, shaking his head until drops of water flew in all directions. He looked cute. Happy. James, who was quieter than his younger brother, dropped on the sand beside her.

"Did you have fun?"

"Yes. I'm hungry."

Caroline pulled out cookies and drinks. She expected Marsh to shift, but he flopped onto the sand beside her.

"Don't you want a drink?"

Marsh stretched closer and licked her hand, a grunt emerging from deep in his throat. She didn't understand his response. He wriggled closer and nudged her hand with his head, then waited, those bright green eyes of his communicating expectation.

Enlightenment came slowly, but she understood. He wanted her to touch him. While she sensed he wouldn't hurt her—he'd never struck her in the time they'd known each other, so there was no reason for him to start now—her hand trembled.

Her hand slid over the top of his head, and when nothing happened, she repeated the careful slide of fingers over his wet fur. With daring, she scratched behind his ears and he tilted his head to give her better access. A rumbling purr sounded, and surprised, her fingers stilled.

"Daddy is purring," James said.

Caroline's head jerked up to study her sons, her cheeks heating. For a second there, she'd forgotten their presence.

"I love Daddy," Ricky said and threw himself at Marsh. He giggled when Marsh licked his cheek.

Marsh and the other black cats drying their fur on the lakeshore didn't scare James or Ricky.

"Have you seen cats before?" Caroline asked Ricky.

"At school we learned cats," Ricky said. "I like cats lots and lots."

"That's good." Something else to ask Marsh.

James shivered, and she glanced at Marsh. "Should we go? The boys look cold." Around them other families were packing up to return to their homes.

Marsh stood and shifted. Ignoring the fine white sand clinging to his skin, he pulled on his jeans and sat on a nearby log to don his boots.

Caroline dressed the boys, and they set off home. Although her life had taken a sudden right-hand turn, this afternoon had been one of the best she could remember.

They didn't talk until after the boys were in bed.

"Are you okay with me sleeping in here with you?" Marsh asked.

"Yes. I know you won't hurt me. I might pester you with questions though, and I'm still confused. A little angry."

Marsh puffed out a breath, the tension residing in his shoulders lifting. At least she was willing to listen. After seeing Caroline's initial reaction he'd thought she might prove difficult. Saul had scared her, but she'd calmed down. The boys were fine. Ricky wanted to know when he could shift to a cat. He'd been very disappointed to learn that it wouldn't happen until he reached his teenage years.

James seemed equally excited and their secret exposure throughout the week had helped ease Caroline. Not that he'd known the school syllabus included feline history. It made sense since there weren't any human children in the class. The more the children knew the better for them to find their place in this modern world.

157

Marsh stripped and crawled into bed. Caroline took longer in the bathroom, and when she shuffled into the bedroom wearing her bright pink wooly slippers, she wore a thick nightgown.

No lovemaking tonight. Marsh sighed, since part of him had been hoping.

"I won't pounce on you, Caroline. All you have to do is say no." His voice came out flatter than he'd intended, with a thin layer of accusation. He swallowed. Damn.

"I was cold," she said, her nose lifting in challenge. "If I was that worried, I would have told you to sleep on the couch."

They stared at each other, turmoil in her gaze that he suspected echoed his.

"I'm sorry," he said in a low voice. "This can't be easy for you. Ask your questions. I'll answer anything you want to ask me, but know this up front. I want you. Our marriage. I want a future with you and our children."

She nodded and kicked off her slippers. She hesitated a fraction longer and whisked her nightgown over her head before climbing into bed.

That small act, one of courage on her part since her immersion into an unknown truth, eased some of the pressure on his chest. He blew out a breath. "I can warm you."

She slid across the width of the bed and into his arms. His feline gave a loud purr and Marsh did nothing to halt the catlike sound.

"You've made that sound ever since I met you."

"Yes, it's my feline part. He loves you as much as I do." God, he'd have to tell her about the mark. No more secrets. "Caroline, I need to tell you something else, something I did a few nights ago."

She froze in his embrace, then pulled back to study his face. "What?"

He swallowed, nerves, the like of which he'd never experienced before, tromped across his stomach lining. A sweat broke out on his brow, and he swallowed for a second time, his feline snarling.

She started, and he realized the sound had squeezed free and wasn't just in his head.

"Sorry. My feline is agitated. Let me explain. When a feline finds his mate, he marks her, biting her on the marking site, the fleshy pad where the neck and shoulder meet."

Her hand crept up to the spot, her fingers massaging the tiny raised scar his bite had left. "You marked me."

"Yes. I...I couldn't help myself. From the moment I met you, I wanted you. My feline recognized something in you and drove me. I wasn't unhappy when you became pregnant."

"Why didn't you tell me at the start? We married, had a child on the way. Why didn't you tell me the truth then?"

Marsh flopped over on his back and stared at the ceiling. "My parents. They didn't want me to marry you. They've always been against matches with humans and were outspoken when Saber mated with Emily. But they couldn't turn their backs on a child who would be a shifter, so we made a deal. They let us live in the farm cottage as long as I kept our feline shapeshifter status secret and didn't mate with you.

"In hindsight, it was a stupid decision because it set us up to be at my parents' beck-and-call. But neither of us had any money, and we had James on the way. I thought it was the only choice, and I still felt guilty about Angus's death. I made a mistake and Angus died. My parents have never let me forget that." Marsh stopped talking and turned his head to glance at Caroline. She was still fingering her mark, and the sight had an immediate reaction. His cock filled and lengthened.

"Knowing your parents, I can understand your decision. I talked to Isabella this afternoon. She helped me see the alternatives."

"Which are?"

"I walk away from you and the boys or I stay."

Marsh flinched at the reality. "Any children we have will inherit the feline gene."

"Yes, which means as a human I don't have the knowledge of how to help them when the shapeshifter gene takes over. In their teens?"

"Yes, I shifted for the first time when I turned thirteen." Marsh glanced at her as a thought occurred. "Occasionally, a shapeshifter will shift at an earlier age."

"When?"

"Sylvie Mitchell shifted for the first time at age five. That was just before Felix and Tomasine came here. It was safer for them."

"Shit," Caroline said. "I don't want to think about our children shifting early. Are there signs?"

"Yes. Our bones start aching and we dream of cats."

Caroline frowned at his words. "I guess if we know what to look for. You'll explain to the boys?"

"Yes. I'll talk to James because he's the same age as Sylvie. I don't think Ricky will understand yet."

Caroline nodded. "Isabella told me someone wanted to kill Tomasine. She also told me about Lisa Jordan and her human stalkers."

"It's Mitchell now. She mated with Sam Mitchell, Saber's cousin."

"I think Isabella's point was that it doesn't matter if we're human or shifter, we can still be in danger. There are some strange people in this world."

"Yes. My parents aren't warm and fuzzy."

Caroline barked out a laugh. "I'm glad we came to live at Glenshee."

"Me too. It's easy to see that the boys love it."

"Yes. Tell me more about the mark since I have one. What does it mean?"

"It's a signal to other male shifters that tells them you're claimed. It ties me to you emotionally. Physically too, I guess. It's made you more disposed to stay with me and the enzymes that I passed to you during the bite will help you live longer."

"How long do you live?"

"Longer than a human. One hundred and thirty years, sometimes longer. Our appearance changes more slowly than a human. We can still die in severe accidents and diseases such as cancer can kill us, but on the whole we're healthier than the average human."

"How do you get on when your official age is over a hundred? Don't people notice?"

Marsh frowned. "I don't know. I've never thought about it, but I suppose the Feline council deals with that sort of thing."

"You have a Feline council?"

"Yes, they're the ones who organized the Middlemarch ball and have started the new activities around the town. The craft market, the upcoming zombie run, the padlock fence. They raised the funds to build the new sports field and changing rooms. It's the feline elders who are on the council. You remember Sid?" At her nod, he continued. "Saber Mitchell is on the council. He's the youngest member. He took over from his Uncle Herbert."

"I can't believe I never noticed. You did shift, I presume?"

"Yes, but I stayed in human form on the farm."

"I feel so stupid."

Marsh rolled over without warning, pushing her flat on the bed and caging her with his strength. She blinked up at him, her blue eyes widening. "You are my mate. You are not stupid. We are a secretive race and have thousands of years of hiding our identity from those who would use us. I promise you—none of the shifters at Glenshee are laughing at you. If anything, it's me who is receiving their censure."

When she didn't reply, he dipped his head to steal a tentative kiss. For a second, Caroline didn't respond and his heart clenched in disappointment, then her arms crept around his neck, holding him to her. Relief filled him along with a purr that vibrated his lips.

Caroline's giggle remained trapped in their kiss as he took control, tasting and teasing her until she moaned. One hand caressed her neck, his callused fingers strumming her mark.

"Marsh," she whispered in a thick voice. "That feels so good. I always wondered why you kept nipping me there."

"My feline trying to exert control," he said. "You don't know how many times I wanted to claim you as my mate. It didn't seem right when you didn't understand."

"But you marked me this week."

"I know. I want to say I'm sorry, but I'm not. Does it make me a prick when I say I love seeing the mark there? It makes me want to puff out my chest and strut."

She laughed. "Why does a puffer pigeon come to my mind when you say that?"

Marsh growled, allowing his feline to emerge without restraint. "Don't insult me, woman. I'm a black leopard shifter."

"Can I mark you?"

"Yes, but it won't leave a mark like yours—at least I don't think so," he added with a frown. "You need to ask Emily and Saber."

"Or I could experiment." She fluttered her eyelashes at him, the action filling him with joy. He thought Caroline might accept him, his otherness, after all.

"Kitten, experiment on me anytime."

"How hard should I bite?"

"I heal fast, and the mark always heals rapidly. Yours did."

"Yes, I expected to have a sore spot the next morning. It surprised me when I didn't."

"And it's best to bite during sex, during climax if possible."

"Okay." She pushed him off her and crawled to the bottom of the bed. Before he could ask, she grasped his cock and slid her hands up and down his shaft. Her mouth closed around his tip and he gasped.

"Christ, woman. Don't bite me there."

He felt the shudder of laughter in her body, then she sucked and licked, sending his mind in an entirely different direction.

Chapter 10

Truth Heals

Caroline's mind reeled with the new knowledge, jumping one way and then the other like a disoriented person in a maze. The one constant she kept returning to was her love for Marsh and their children. None of them were monsters, even with their otherness. Yes, everything else was secondary, and she'd settle her thoughts in the coming days. Just one day at a time.

Instead of stressing, she gave herself over to loving Marsh. She stroked. She sucked. She licked until his big body trembled and his balls tightened and lifted. Judging he was almost ready to come, she pulled her mouth off him and straddled his legs. In seconds, she lifted over him and impaled herself, taking him easily. She rode him at a lazy pace, pleasing herself and watching his face the entire time.

Handsome. Striking. His green eyes blazed with passion, his too-long black hair spread over the pillow. He gripped her hips as he encouraged her to move faster. Since it was what she wanted, she allowed the increase in pace. Something pierced her hip, and she realized he'd grown claws, which fascinated her.

She saw he was struggling for control, yet trying to be gentle with her, and this knowledge made her go mushy inside. She used one hand to stroke her clit while she continued her rapid rise and fall. Then, she was hurtling into ecstasy, white-hot pleasure rippling down her legs and blazing upward to her chest. The spasms took over, and Marsh moved with speed. He flipped her over and plunged deep. One stroke. Two. Then he stilled, balls-deep in her, a shudder speeding through his entire body. He fingered her mark and her pussy pulsed around his girth, squeezing another spasm of pleasure free.

For an instant, he rested his weight on her, his forehead touching hers.

"Thank you, Caroline," he whispered, and she knew he was thanking her for way more than the passionate loving. She stroked her hand over his back, enjoying the closeness, both mentally and physically.

"I forgot to bite you."

"We have plenty of time, kitten."

"I always wondered why you called me that. Now it makes sense."

"You're everything I need, everything my feline needs. To us you're our kitten."

Damn. She dragged in a breath, aware of the shift between them. Damn if he didn't make her want to purr.

A new openness sprang to life with the employees of Glenshee during the next week, and part of Caroline wondered how she'd been so blind. Now that she knew, she could see the small clues she should have noticed, but had swept aside as quirky or odd. She often came across men in half dress, with no clothes or in feline form.

Marsh had caught her gaping at two of the men and gone all alpha. She kneaded her batch of bread and grinned at the memory of her husband, her mate, ordering the men not to come into the kitchen unless they had their pants on or wore fur. His mate didn't need to see their nudity, just his.

"Hey, Knife Lady." Caroline turned at the teasing shout from the door. "Is it safe to come in? I've come to collect the lunches."

Saul spluttered from where he stood at the stove, stirring a white sauce for the fish pie they'd decided on for part of the dinner.

Caroline rolled her eyes. "The lunches are over there on the counter in that box. Come inside and take your chances."

Saul cocked his head. "We have a visitor."

"I'll check." Maxwell, the guy who picked up the lunches, strode away.

"I'm envious of your hearing," Caroline said. "I can't hear a thing."

"At least you don't have to smell half of what we can. Ladies who overdo the perfume are hideous. I sneeze and pretend to have allergies. Some guys with aftershave too."

"I hadn't thought of that."

"Visitors for you," Maxwell said, striding into the kitchen.

"Me?" Caroline noticed he scanned her for a knife, and she cackled. "Knife. Just over there."

Maxwell froze, the color leaving his face.

Saul chuckled. "She's teasing you, man."

Maxwell blushed, the tips of his ears turning pink as he picked up the chiller-bag of lunches and left.

Caroline heard him speak and the next minute, Emily, Tomasine and Isabella crowded into the kitchen.

"Saul," Emily said. "I didn't know you were here."

"I arrived without warning, and stayed to help Caroline."

"It was his fault I learned about feline shapeshifters before Marsh told me," Caroline said.

Saul winked at Caroline. "She pulled a knife, prepared to gut me to save her kids from the big mean leopard."

Emily slapped her hand over her mouth to cut off her laugh. Above her hand, her eyes danced with merriment.

"You didn't?" Tomasine asked, and Caroline could tell she was trying not to laugh too.

Caroline nodded. "I did. Let me put this bread in the oven and I'll make us a morning tea."

"I'm glad you stayed," Isabella said. "I thought you would. You're strong."

Caroline glanced at her. "Your bluntness regarding my options pulled me up and made me think about what I wanted and everything I'd have to give up."

"How are the boys taking it?" Tomasine asked.

Caroline placed six loaves of bread into the big oven and set the timer. She washed her hands and filled the jug to make tea and coffee. "With scarcely a blink. They'd seen and learned things since they'd been here. They never mentioned anything, but I'd noticed their fascination with leopards. Ricky keeps asking when he will turn into a cat. He's obsessed with leopards and loves to play with the men when they're in leopard form."

"Grab a seat at the table," Saul said. "I'll make tea and coffee for you. We're way ahead. Spend time with your friends."

"Thanks." She turned to Isabella. "Since Saul has been helping in the kitchen I've had the afternoons to sew. Your dress is almost finished, apart from the hem. Normally, I'd do two fittings, but I didn't know when I'd see you, so I kept going. Tomasine, your dress is done too, and Emily's is underway."

"Did Isabella tell you about the market?" Emily asked.

"A little."

"It was brilliant." Tomasine's eyes sparkled. "People crowded the hall, and since it was a warm day, we had a few stalls selling food and drinks, set up outside. Most of the stallholders sold out, and the Feline council is thrilled with the funds we raised."

"When is the next one?" Caroline asked. "Maria and Cam are back soon. Once Maria is back, I'll have more time since I'll only be helping her a few hours each day."

Saul placed the teapot on the table and returned with mugs, milk and sugar, and a plate of cheese scones, not long out of the oven He set a pot of coffee in front of her.

"Yum," Isabella said. "Cheese scones are my favorite."

"You've lost weight," Emily said. "Have they been working you hard?"

"It hasn't been so bad since Saul arrived to help. After cooking food all day, I haven't wanted to eat."

"I get that." Emily reached for a scone. "It's nice to eat food other people have cooked."

"You look great, Caroline." Tomasine cocked her head and studied her. "There is a sparkle to you that wasn't there before."

"I am happy," Caroline said. "We haven't been here long, but it has been the right move for all of us. Marsh is happier too, and for once, we have money in the bank."

"I heard that Charles and Dawn lost their new farmhand yesterday." Isabella sipped her black tea. "He's had trouble getting replacement workers."

Caroline sighed. "He always found fault with anything Marsh did. It's easy to see the difference in Marsh now, and we're able to spend more time together as a family."

A yeasty fresh-bread aroma mingled with the onions Saul was browning as he made a quiche.

"It's lovely to see you," Caroline said. "Are you staying the night? It's a long drive here and back to Middlemarch."

"We'll drive part of the way back and stay at a bed and breakfast," Emily said. "It's nice to have a break."

"Who is looking after the café?" Caroline buttered a scone and took a bite.

"My two local ladies," Emily said.

"Dara, one of the women here, wondered if she could sell her knitting. She says that during the winter, when Glenshee is cut off, she spends her time knitting and her family doesn't need any more jumpers or scarves. She said the other women knit and crochet. What do you think?" Caroline smiled. "I could even design a Glenshee label for us to use."

Emily and Tomasine glanced at each other, excitement in their grins.

"Any other sewers?" Isabella asked.

"No. One of the ladies spins wool. Dara uses the wool to knit her projects."

"I think that is a fantastic idea," Emily said.

Tomasine nodded. "Especially the label."

"I don't mind selling the stuff for you," Isabella offered. "It was fun. I can buy supplies for any of you. Actually, that was part of my idea. I know you don't have spare cash at present, but I wondered if you'd let me buy fabric, cotton, buttons and zippers for you, so you'll have plenty to keep you busy during the winter. You could give me a small cut for selling after we take out the price of the supplies."

Caroline nodded. "I love sewing and designing, but I don't want to become a production line."

"I thought of that," Isabella said. "If you give me a general guide as to what you want, then when the stuff arrives at

Glenshee, you can make whatever you want. Buyers snapped up the dresses and children's shirts. I didn't get to try my sales pitch."

"She didn't," Tomasine said with a grin. "She'd practiced it on me."

"I agree with Isabella." Emily chuckled when Isabella pulled a face at Tomasine. "You could use your design skills. We had a crowd of varied ages, thrilled to have something like this in the country. Once the word gets around we'll have even more people attending."

"The part that slows me is sewing on buttons and hemming. I can do hems with my machine but some need to be done by hand."

"Teach me," Isabella said. "If I can sew a wound shut, I can sew on a button. I'll check with Leo, but I could stay a few days. Leo was saying he'd love to visit Glenshee since Felix has told him so much about the station. He'll be thrilled at the opportunity. What do you say?"

"You can stay in the main house," Saul said from the other side of the kitchen. "Cam and Maria won't mind."

The women stared at her. Emily and Tomasine both wore smiles while Isabella's expression remained blank.

Caroline liked Isabella. She liked all three women who had befriended her. "I love the idea."

"I don't mind helping with buttons and things," Tomasine said. "Isabella can show me."

"What wounds have you treated?" Caroline demanded.

Isabella gave a sly smile. "I'll tell you while you teach me."

"Don't scare her," Tomasine ordered.

"I'd never do that to a friend," Isabella said, and when she smiled, Caroline noted her teeth appeared pointier. "Only enemies should fear me."

Emily spluttered while Caroline just gaped at her.

"Isabella," Tomasine said, and a chiding note colored the petite woman's voice.

Isabella tossed her head. "I purchased fabric just in case you said yes. Do you want to see?" A diffidence appeared in her then, and Caroline realized she wasn't as confident as she projected.

"I'd love it. It will be just like Christmas."

Isabella beamed.

"After lunch," Saul announced. "The men will be here soon."

Caroline stood. "I'd better set the table. Dara will arrive with the boys any minute."

"I'll show Emily and Isabella around," Tomasine said. "I'd love to see Dara and the others while we're here. We can bring your boys back for you."

Caroline agreed, and the women left while she and Saul prepared for the six hungry men who would arrive any minute.

"They like you," Saul said.

"I haven't known them long. Not properly. Marsh and I didn't go out much, so most of the Middlemarch residents were only nodding acquaintances."

"They're good women. They'll be good friends you can trust."

173

"I'm figuring that out. Are you sure it will be okay for Isabella to stay at the homestead?"

"Sure. Maria and Cam are easygoing."

"Does she have a knife?" someone called.

Saul snorted. "Sounds as if the comedians have arrived for lunch. Let's both pick up a knife."

Caroline grinned and turned to find her weapon of choice.

"Come to bed, kitten," Marsh said.

"There's not enough room for this fabric." She planted her hands on her hips as she surveyed the mess.

"When Cam and Maria arrive home, I'll ask if there is a place you can set up your machine and organize your sewing. They might have an empty cottage or an idea we haven't considered."

"You'd do that?"

"Kitten. Of course, I'd do that for you. I want you to be happy and sewing pleases you. I know you regretted giving up your course at varsity, and I love seeing you so animated about a project. I watched you at dinner tonight, discussing sewing and knitting and the market. This idea excites you. It's good for you and all the funds that pour into the Feline council help the shapeshifter community. I can't see any downside."

"I'm lucky to have you. Some men don't like—"

"I think I'm the lucky one. Bed," he repeated. "I don't know about you, but I'm tired."

Caroline went to him and kissed his brow. "I guess staying out overnight watching for sheep rustlers is tiring."

Marsh yawned. "Bloody glad it's not my turn tonight."

"Do you think they'll come again?"

"Hamish thinks so, and he's in charge when Cam isn't here."

She let Marsh guide her toward their bedroom. "You get ready for bed. I'll check on the boys first."

"They're both asleep. Ricky is snoring."

"Now I have to check to see if you're right."

"I'll do the I-told-you-so when you get in bed," Marsh said with a yawn.

"Go to bed. I'll be there in a minute." Before he could argue, she trotted down the passage toward the boys' rooms.

James had curled up in a ball, his breathing steady. She resettled the blankets around his form and gave in to the urge to touch, brushing his curls off his forehead. A wave of love filled her, and she knew she'd made the right decision. She could never leave her children, no matter what genes they carried.

And Marsh...

She smiled into the darkness and stood.

Ricky was snoring, his limbs twitching as if he were running. Of their two children, he'd been the most excited about turning into a cat. James drew black leopards, but Ricky had run around growling at everyone.

Marsh laughed and said he'd grow out of it. This was new to him.

Caroline resettled the covers Ricky had kicked off and leaned over to kiss his brow. Satisfied, the boys were settled, she returned to their bedroom. Marsh was also snoring. A grin curled her lips. There would be teasing tomorrow. She partially closed their door, leaving it ajar so she could hear if either of the boys needed them and pulled off her clothes.

She was tired herself, her muscles aching from lugging around boxes of fabrics. Emily and Tomasine had left and she and Isabella had gone through the boxes of supplies she'd purchased. It would be like having her own shop, and already her mind spun designs. She hadn't felt this enthusiastic about sewing and designing for a long time.

Although she'd protested the cost, Isabella had waved the subject away. She had funds, she'd said, that she didn't know how to spend and this investment was gold.

"Besides, learning how to sew buttons and hems and anything else you need done will give me more purpose. I help Emily in the café, but I need to do other stuff."

Curiosity had propelled Caroline to ask, "What did you do before you came to Middlemarch?"

"I was an assassin." She delivered this in a flat tone that from any other person Caroline would have cried fib.

"Truth?"

Isabella nodded, treating Caroline like a nervous animal that might flee at any second. "Ask Tomasine."

"I suppose there aren't many job openings for an assassin in Middlemarch."

"No, that's why I'm looking for something to fill my time."

"Do you know any martial arts?"

"Yes."

"Get your teaching certificate or whatever you need to teach and hold classes for the kids. In the country, there aren't many opportunities for the kids. They'd love something like that. You could run classes for all ages. The local women might enjoy learning self-defense or you could run a fitness class. I'm sure there are situations where it is best for shifters to remain in human form. Discuss it with your Feline council."

"You are a genius," Isabella said. "I'll talk to Saber."

"I presume an assassin needs to keep fit. You could do a boot camp fitness class. Rugby is starting and people will want to get in training for the zombie run."

Isabella had grabbed her in a hug and kissed her square on the mouth, shocking Caroline into silence. Saul had laughed hard enough to bust a gut. Caroline slid into bed, smiling at the memory.

"Why are you smiling?"

"Isabella kissed me today."

"What?" Marsh sounded more awake.

"She was excited about the ideas I suggested. I think she's bored and needs things to keep her busy."

"That's okay then. Leo is my friend. I'd hate to tell him our mates have run off together. I wouldn't like it either."

"Good to know," she said and snuggled closer.

A growl woke her. High-pitched and loud, right next to her ear. Groggy from sleep, Caroline turned her head, trying to escape. Something furry brushed against her cheek, her eyes flicked open and she screamed, rolling from bed and getting tangled in the covers. She toppled to the floor, her gaze on the fluffy black cat quivering near her pillow. Its green eyes were big and wide, and it let out a cry.

Marsh came running from the bathroom, a towel around his waist. He scooped up the cat and held it, stroking along its spine until the animal purred.

Caroline slapped her hand over her yawn. "Where did it come from? James and Ricky must have sneaked it inside."

"Back in a minute," Marsh said in a terse voice.

Caroline picked herself up off the floor and pulled on her dressing gown. She stuffed her feet in her slippers just as Marsh appeared, the cat still in his arms.

Caroline frowned at the fluffy black bundle. It purred like a motor boat with each stroke of Marsh's fingers. "It's big for a domestic cat."

"You'd better take a seat," Marsh said, a strange expression on his face.

"Why? James? Ricky? Is something wrong?"

James appeared behind Marsh, his black curls sticking up at right angles. That answered part of her question.

"Ricky?"

"This is Ricky," Marsh said.

"What? But..." Caroline parked her butt on the corner of their bed, her knees giving out on her. "I don't understand. I thought only teenagers..." She stared at the purring cat—leopard—in Marsh's arms. Her mouth worked but not a sound emerged.

Marsh stroked Ricky, and their son purred louder, lifting his head, so Marsh could stroke under his chin.

"How?" she asked. "Will he change back?"

"In theory," Marsh said, his gaze on her.

"Theory?"

"He's only three. I've never heard of children shifting this early, not apart from Sylvie."

Caroline puffed out a breath. "Sylvie is okay."

"I...hell." Marsh set Ricky on the bed beside Caroline and Ricky sidled up to her. Automatically, she stroked his back and soon his loud rumbly purrs filled the bedroom.

"Marsh, what aren't you telling me?"

"He's three. Getting him to understand how to shift might be more difficult than it was with Sylvie. Felix told me, the shift terrified her, and he worried she wouldn't shift back. The first shift is painful."

Caroline understood everything Marsh didn't state aloud. Ricky had to want to shift back to his human form, and given

Ricky's disappointment at not being able to shift until he was a teenager plus the pain angle, their son might stay in feline form.

"Can you talk to him?"

"I'll do my best," Marsh promised.

James sidled closer and climbed on the bed, his eyes wide. "Wow."

"Yes," Caroline said dryly.

Ricky gave her hand a nudge because she'd stopped patting him.

"It's time to get moving." Marsh scooped up Ricky.

Caroline watched them leave, fear swooping through her belly.

"Is that Ricky?" James asked.

"Yes," Caroline said. "Don't you dare copy him, James Rutherford. This is not a contest."

"I can draw him."

Caroline exhaled, aware she'd been sharp with her son. "Yes, of course you can. Ask Daddy to take photos for you. Ricky will be in his human form soon."

She hoped.

Chapter 11

Feline Drama

On automatic pilot, Caroline grabbed a box of breakfast cereal from the pantry and plonked it on the kitchen table. She put on the jug and walked to a cupboard to get out plates. Her son—her three-year-old son had transformed into a leopard.

James entered the kitchen, then she heard a growl and the clack of claws against the tiled kitchen floor. She turned from the cutlery drawer in time to see Ricky leap at James's back. Her oldest son landed with a crash, sending a chair toppling to the floor.

Ricky put his furry head close to James's and growled, white teeth flashing.

"Ricky!" Caroline darted closer to grab Ricky, and he bared his teeth at her. Undeterred, she reached out to seize him by the scruff, and her son clawed her, hissing and spitting when James attempted to struggle free.

Caroline winced as her breaths sawed in and out and the pain kicked in. She gaped at the lines of blood that formed on her forearm.

"Ricky." Marsh's tone was harsh and growly. "Let James up."

Ricky continued to hiss and spit, and Marsh moved so fast, Caroline blinked. He grabbed Ricky by the scruff and held him up, then roared at his son in a feline manner. There was an instant of stunned silence then Ricky went limp in Marsh's grip. He gave a tiny whimper, and Marsh placed him on the floor.

"Stay there," Marsh snapped.

Ricky sat and shook.

Caroline glanced away from the blood beaded on her arm, feeling lightheaded. Marsh murmured to James and helped him to stand.

"Start your breakfast while I fix your mum's arm. Can you get your cereal?"

"Yes, Daddy."

Caroline groaned. There would be cereal all over the table.

Marsh crouched beside her where she still sat on the floor. "Are you okay?" He surveyed the scratch marks. "He got you good."

"Yeah. He frightened me." Tears swam in her eyes, reaction setting in. Frightened of her own son.

"It won't happen again. If he misbehaves, you must tell me."

"I will," she promised.

"Let's get you cleaned up." Marsh helped her up and led her to the bathroom.

"You realize James will spill cereal everywhere."

"He might surprise us." Marsh washed off the blood and studied the wound. "It's not too bad. You don't need stitches."

Caroline felt her mouth drop open. Shock slapped her as the truth of his words dawned. "You mean he could have injured me worse?"

"Yes." Marsh's tone was grim. "I'll lay down the law with him. If you have problems, get an adult to snarl at him. There is a hierarchy in a shifter leap. Elders get respect and Ricky will have to learn that. It's a natural process of learning, but Ricky is doing things differently."

"Mum! Mum!"

"Just a minute, James," Marsh called. "I'll put on iodine spray and plasters."

"Have we got colored ones? I need to help Saul in the kitchen as soon as Dara collects James. And figure out what to do with Ricky."

"Mum! Dad!" James shouted.

She and Marsh hurried along the passage to the kitchen.

"What is it?" Marsh demanded.

"Look what Ricky did," James said and pointed.

Ricky sat on the kitchen floor beside a large puddle.

"Oh, heck," Caroline said. "And I thought it couldn't get any worse."

T wo days later, Ricky remained in feline form, and Caroline was at her wits end. His early shift fascinated the other feline residents at Glenshee. They didn't have to clean up the puddles on the floor—toileting mishaps—or deal with the other problems created by a young feline. He kept using his claws on the walls and furniture, then there was meal time. It didn't seem right giving him cereal and milk or porridge.

James sat at their table, eating his breakfast while Ricky ate chopped steak from a bowl. Once finished, Ricky trotted over to her and wound between her legs, purring loudly.

"Ricky, are you going to shift today? Remember what Daddy told you about shifting?"

Marsh had spoken to Ricky and described the shifting process. By now, even Caroline knew to imagine her form and concentrate to start a shift from feline to human.

Ricky cocked his head and ran to the door. As usual, he ignored the instructions, seeming happy in feline form.

Marsh arrived home, exhausted after keeping watch over a flock of sheep. "Hey." He kissed her, ruffled James's hair and stooped to pet Ricky.

"I think you should send him to school with James," Marsh said.

"Will he be safe?"

A tap sounded on the door seconds before it opened. Isabella sauntered into the kitchen. Dara arrived seconds later to collect James for school.

"I think you should keep him to a routine," Isabella said, not even pretending she hadn't eavesdropped.

Marsh sank onto a chair at the kitchen table. "Hopefully he'll miss the things he used to do as a human and shift on his own."

Caroline eyed her younger son. "The next time he makes a puddle on the floor, I will rub his nose in it."

A gurgle escaped Isabella, and she slapped her hand over her mouth.

"I hadn't thought of the practicalities," Dara said, her lips twitching as she fought a smile.

Caroline snorted. "I'm living them. What do you think, Dara? Will Ricky be okay at school?"

"I think it's a good idea. He might miss painting or the other activities and want to join in with the other kids his age. There are always other mothers helping out."

Caroline nodded. "Ricky."

He trotted over to her, and she knelt to speak with him eye to eye. "Dara will take you to school. If you need to go to the toilet, walk to the door and snarl, so the teacher knows to let you outside. All right?"

"I'll have a word with the teacher," Dara promised.

Ricky grunted and stalked to Marsh. He sat on his haunches and looked stubborn.

Caroline sighed and stood. "He thinks that now he is a feline, he should work on the farm with the others." She scooped him up and spoke sternly. "You will go to school today, so you turn out smart like your daddy. The other shifters went to school

185

to learn how to work on the farm." She had no idea if she spoke the truth, but it was time for firmness. "If you go to school this morning, I'll ask Saul if he will take you running this afternoon."

"Leo arrives today. We'll take Ricky out, if Saul can't." Isabella scratched Ricky behind his ears. "But only if you behave and go to school this morning."

That solution found favor with Ricky and he trotted after James and Dara.

"I came to tell you that Cam rang this morning," Isabella said.

"How is Maria?" Caroline asked.

"She's fine. They're taking an extra week to spend time in Auckland. I asked Cam if we could use a room for your sewing materials. Maria said you can set up in the small reception room on the other side of the main lounge. She also said that she wants in on the market project. She used to sew as a teenager and would enjoy starting again. According to Cam, she has always wanted to change the reception room into a hobby room. Saul said he'd help us with shelves."

"When is Maria going to have time to sew?"

"Ah, that was the other thing. She has decided to hire more help in the kitchen. The break has made her realize she needs more help," Isabella said. "Cam is pleased."

"Sounds perfect," Marsh said and yawned.

"Catch a couple of hours sleep," Caroline ordered. "Isabella and I will move this sewing stuff back to the main homestead."

"I brought the ute," Isabella said, referring to the farm utility vehicle. "I figured it would be easier to shift everything at once."

The morning flew with both Isabella and Caroline working in the kitchen with Saul, then moving to the new sewing room. With dual aspect windows, there was plenty of natural light. Saul had found shelving from somewhere and fixed it to one wall.

Isabella stacked bolts of material on the shelves while Caroline sorted out the cotton and haberdashery.

The patter of feet and scramble of claws announced Dara's arrival with James, Ricky and her brood. Caroline strode toward the kitchen and found Saul sneaking the children a warm cookie each.

Ricky let out a protesting yowl because he hadn't received a cookie. Saul glanced at her, and she shrugged.

"I have no idea if he should eat them or not." Caroline frowned. "I wouldn't have a problem if he was in human form." She took a chocolate chip cookie and crouched to give it to her son. His black fluffy coat bore splotches of Irish-green paint. The side of his face sported crimson. "You need a bath."

Ricky grabbed the cookie and sprinted around the table.

"Don't worry," Isabella said in an undertone. "We'll do some of our running along the edge of the lake. The water will wash off the paint. A car. It's Leo." Her face brightened, and she sprinted for the door.

"James, do you want to help decorate cookies this afternoon? Saul is making gingerbread men."

Cookie finished, Ricky trotted back around the table and stopped in front of her. He yowled.

Caroline made a clucking sound of disappointment. "I'm sorry, Ricky. You can only help with the gingerbread men if you have hands."

Ricky stared up at her, his big green eyes unblinking.

The door opened and Leo and Isabella wandered inside. Ricky trotted over to Isabella and when she didn't pay any attention to him, he bit her calf.

Before Caroline could remonstrate him, Isabella seized him by the scruff.

"No biting. If you don't say sorry, I won't take you for a run."

Ricky made a pitiful sound and when she set him back on the floor, he licked her hand.

"Who is this?" Leo asked, curiosity filling his handsome face.

"My three-year-old son, Ricky," Caroline said. "No matter how much we talk to him and explain how to change back, he refuses to listen."

"Three?" Leo tracked Ricky as he stalked across the kitchen floor and jumped on an intrepid bug. "Hell."

"Succinct. That's my mate," Isabella said. "I promised I'd take Ricky for a run. We're stopping via the lake to have a...swim. You want to come?"

"Sure," Leo said. "I could do with a run."

Caroline swallowed, a sudden tightness to her throat and chest. She blinked and realized she was on the verge of crying.

The sound of crying—Caroline's crying—halted Marsh at the entrance of their cottage. Fear and anxiety tightened his breath and his feline grabbed for control. His head drooped before he straightened. He'd hidden from the truth long enough. Probably the reason for her tears. He strode into the kitchen, glanced around for the boys. They weren't there.

"Caroline? What's wrong?" He wanted to go to her, wanted to tug her into his arms, but the sight of her tear-stained face had him sweating, his hands trembling. "Is it Ricky? James?"

"No, they're fine. James is decorating cookies with Saul, and Isabella and Leo took Ricky for a run. I just—" She rose from the wooden chair and flung herself at him.

A wave of relief engulfed him. So much relief. He wrapped his arms around her and held her tight, soothing both himself and his feline. "I thought...I thought you were having second thoughts."

Caroline pushed back and stared up at him, her face blotchy, her eyes red from crying, yet he'd never seen anyone so beautiful.

"No! No second thoughts. If anything, I'm glad it happened while we were here where everyone understands. Imagine if Ricky had shifted while we were living in Middlemarch."

"He wouldn't have had the idea to shift if we were still in Middlemarch."

"Maybe." Caroline sighed and burrowed against his chest again. "I'm just so scared. Ricky doesn't want to change back.

He's enjoying himself too much as a kitten. What if he stays like that?"

"He might." Marsh knew that wasn't what she wanted to hear, but he didn't intend to lie. "All we can do is show him he'll miss out on things if he stays in feline form. All of us have described how to shift and encouraged him."

She stepped back to study his face. "I've heard the workers asking him if he knows. He stares with those big green eyes and purrs. Damn it, I don't want to install a cat flap."

Marsh barked out a laugh, then sobered. "It might come to that."

"This isn't funny. I'm worried about Ricky."

"So am I. Look, Caroline. All we can do is what we're already doing. We have to wait until Ricky decides he wants to change back to human."

A tear dripped down her cheek. "Oh, Marsh. What are we going to do if he never changes back?"

"Try not to worry, kitten. We'll take each day one at a time."

She nodded and frowned. "Why are you at home this time of the day?"

"Alan was meant to watch for the stock thieves tonight. Something in the paddock has given him allergies, and he can't stop sneezing. Hamish asked if I'd take over for him. He sent me home to have a sleep."

"I didn't sleep much last night."

"Come and lie down with me. We're both exhausted. Saul, Isabella and Leo will make sure the kids are all right."

The afternoon nap with Caroline had done Marsh good. He'd thought they might make love, but they'd both fallen asleep and hadn't woken until Isabella arrived with the boys. Marsh smiled into the darkness, even as he scanned the landscape shrouded with darkness. Isabella and Leo had tired Ricky out, and on arriving home, he'd curled into a ball on Marsh's favorite armchair and gone to sleep. Marsh had carried him to bed before he'd left to take over the watch. Ricky hadn't roused from his deep sleep.

Ricky was healthy and had a good appetite. Perhaps that was all that mattered. Marsh considered and smiled. If he, Caroline and James left the station, Ricky couldn't go with them. If he missed out on a few treats, he'd become more amenable to returning to his human form.

The hum of an approaching vehicle caught his attention. His gaze tracked the progress of the farm vehicle and studied it when the driver pulled over and parked on the shoulder of the road. He tugged a phone from his pocket and speed dialed Hamish. "I think we have action. There is a ute pulled up on the shoulder. Guy is getting out. Looks as if he's waiting for someone." Marsh inhaled, testing the air, the prevailing breeze coming toward him. Lucky break. "There are two guys. Smells as if they have dogs."

"It's a private road," Hamish muttered.

"My thoughts exactly. Wait a sec." Marsh cocked his head, hearing the approach of another vehicle, a louder rumble. "Here comes a truck."

"Hang tight. We'll be there in ten minutes. Don't do anything stupid."

"I won't, boss," Marsh said. No way did he intend to confront the thieves. He had too much to live for—Caroline and the boys.

Ricky woke up Caroline by batting her across the face with his paw.

"Ow, mind the claws," Caroline protested as she leaned over to flick on the bedside light. "What's wrong?"

Ricky sprang off the bed and trotted from the bedroom.

"Couldn't you wait an hour?"

Ricky growled, and Caroline stumbled from bed. She could hardly blame him since she'd lectured him about making puddles. She shuffled along the passage and opened the front door.

"Come straight back." She expected Ricky to scamper over to the patch of grass on the other side of the driveway. But Ricky raced down the driveway and headed toward the homestead.

Caroline ran after him and found large black leopards listening to Hamish.

"What is it?" she demanded, coming to a halt by Dara. She kept her gaze on Ricky and saw him cock his head as if he was listening to Hamish too. Surely he didn't think he could go with the men?

"Ricky." She spoke in a stern tone. "Come and stand by me, out of the way."

"What's up?" Isabella asked sliding into a spot near Caroline. Leo stood behind her.

"The sheep thieves have returned." She glanced back at where Ricky had been seconds before and couldn't see him. "Can you see Ricky? He seems to think he should help."

"I see him," Leo said. "I'll go and get him."

"You should get warm clothes," Isabella said. "You're shivering. Hamish, do you want me and Leo to help?" Isabella spoke to the boss when he headed in their direction.

"Yeah, did you bring a gun?"

"Always," Isabella said.

"Might come in handy to have someone in human form to speak for us."

"I'll grab my weapons and follow. How far on foot?"

"Ten minutes for a feline."

Isabella took off at a run.

Caroline scanned the vicinity for Ricky and Leo. "Ricky!"

"Shush, Caroline," Hamish ordered. "Sound carries in the night. I don't want those bastards to get more of our sheep."

"I think Ricky ran off after the men."

"What?"

193

"Ricky—"

"I heard you the first time," he snapped, sounding harried. "Stay here. We'll bring him back."

"You could tell him I intend to think up a nasty punishment."

"Stand in line," Hamish warned as he ripped off his shirt.

Caroline turned away, giving him privacy as he got ready to shift. No matter how many times the men shifted when she was around, she felt weird looking when they stripped. "Hamish, please find Ricky."

Isabella tore past them and Hamish bounded after her. Soon, they blended with the darkness. Caroline stared after them, rubbing her hands over her arms to keep warm. She wanted to follow and search for her son, but retraced her steps to their home. They had enough to concentrate on at present. They didn't need her blundering around in the dark, getting in their way.

When she reached the house, she checked on James. He'd slept through the entire drama. In their bedroom, she pulled on a pair of sweats and a T-shirt. Unable to settle, she put on the kettle to make a cup of milo. Ricky...the little imp was in so much trouble.

Marsh stalked closer to the men, hoping to eavesdrop while they waited for the truck. He'd been right. They had dogs, and they sensed his presence. One of the dogs—he thought there were three—whimpered, and the nearest guy snapped at it to be quiet. Nervous. Good. He could work with that while he waited for the rest of the men to arrive.

He slinked closer, hugging the scant piles of rocks and the tussock clumps.

"Here is the truck now. I'll let out the dogs."

The first man strode to the compartment on the back of the ute, the metal bar holding the door locked sounding loud in the silence. Four dogs jumped free and leaped to the ground.

Once in position, he waited, every muscle tense as he listened to them discuss their plan in low voices.

"Like taking candy off a baby," one scoffed. He appeared older and was smaller in stature.

The dogs milled around, uncertain. They could smell him, but weren't sure of the situation.

"What's wrong with the sheep?" the younger man asked. "They're milling around as if something is out there. Better bring the gun."

The air whistled through the older man's teeth. "Theft of sheep is one thing, but I don't like guns. We don't need them. They have no idea we're here. Let's get the sheep and leave." He whistled, a quiet sound that reached the dogs. They pricked their ears and trotted to their master.

Marsh remained motionless, relaxing a fraction as he heard the low growl from one of his workmates.

"What was that?" the young guy demanded. "Did you hear it?"

"Something out there all right. Don't go waving that gun around, boy. The last thing we want is you shooting wildly in a panic. Someone might get hurt."

The older man whistled at his dogs again, the sound different in tone this time, and the four dogs raced into the darkness toward the uneasy knot of merino sheep.

The truck pulled to a stop, and two men, the driver and passenger, exited the vehicle. They opened the rear of the truck and pulled out poles with quick efficiency.

A mobile yard. The younger man went to help and within five minutes they'd erected a holding yard for the sheep. They'd done this a time or two and Marsh wondered if they'd stolen his father's stock.

The man with the dogs rounded up the sheep and drove them toward the mobile yards. Marsh quivered with the urge to move but stuck with their plan and waited for Hamish's signal to draw in behind the herd of bunched sheep and dogs, to surround the men.

It would be soon.

Hamish's sharp bark of command rang out, echoing in the gully.

"What the hell was that?" one of the men demanded.

"Told Toby there was something out there. I heard stories of big black cats wandering these hills."

"Don't let your imagination get the better of you," a gruff voice commanded. "Boss wants these sheep. He's paying us top dollar, so we're gonna deliver."

Marsh smirked. Wouldn't happen. Not this night.

He rose and crept through the darkness, following the men as they approached the mobile yard.

Hamish called again, and Marsh heard the fury vibrating in his single snarl.

"Something is fuckin' out there, I tell you."

"Put your hands in the air where I can see them or I'll shoot," Isabella said in a clear, firm voice.

"You and whose army, girlie," the younger man with the gun asked, his tone casual. Amused.

Marsh sucked in a breath, hoping this wouldn't end in gunfire, but suspected the situation might head south in a big way.

Marsh kept his gaze on Isabella, caught her wry smile in the scant light.

"I've brought my army," Isabella said.

Hamish barked another order, and they closed up.

"What the fuck?" the young guy with the gun cried. He whipped the gun from the small of his back and fired at one of the leopards.

Marsh heard the grunt of pain, smelled the blood and hoped it wasn't serious. His next shot went wild, then the man gave a terrified shriek, the small gun—Marsh couldn't see what it was—dropping to the ground.

"You shot me," the man cried.

"You're still talking," Isabella countered. "You, line up against the truck. Keep your hands where I can see them. Hamish, you got the guy with the dogs?"

The truck driver tried to make a run for it, and Marsh stalked him. When the man broke into a run, Marsh sprang at him and knocked him off his feet.

The man screamed, tried to scramble free. Marsh planted a paw in the middle of his back and forced the man back to the ground. The man turned his head, and Marsh took satisfaction in his terrified expression. He pushed his face close and snarled, letting his hot breath waft over the man's features.

"Watch it," Isabella's voice came. "Don't run or I'll set my cats on you."

Marsh snorted. *Her cats.* The men would grumble about that later.

"Idiot," Isabella muttered. "Hamish, the guy is running toward you."

Marsh moved off the truck driver, watching him to make sure he remained on the ground. He peered into the darkness where Hamish had stationed himself and gaped.

That wasn't one of the men. A dog? No, they were all over by the sheep and the older guy. Crap, it was Ricky, and he was running straight toward the fleeing man. His throat closed up as panic filled him. He growled, calling for another of the felines. One arrived and Marsh took off, fear propelling him to speed.

Ricky didn't stop. Instead he kept running toward the man, and Marsh saw Leo scrambling after him, still in human form.

The human thief ran blindly, fear propelling him onward. He didn't see Ricky, and Marsh didn't think he even noticed Leo's presence.

Ricky aimed at the man's feet. The collision brought the man down. Ricky howled. The man toppled facedown on the ground. Ricky picked himself up and jumped on the man's back. The man roared with pain. Claws. Ricky wasn't good at sheathing his claws yet.

The man thrashed, arms flying as he turned his body. One arm struck Ricky, sent him flying. He struck the ground with an audible thud.

Ricky didn't get up.

Ricky didn't move.

Chapter 12

Middlemarch Visit

R *icky!*

Marsh screamed, the feline yowl of distress echoing off the surrounding hills.

"Let me look," Leo said. "I'll take care of him."

Marsh heeded the warning. Rumors of black cats would pass as intriguing, but whispers of men changing to big black cats might start people on a hunt for the truth. He had to keep his head. Marsh padded up to the panicked man and bit his arm. It was a nip rather than a bite, but he drew blood. He wanted to do much more. He wanted to damage the thief.

Hamish called out a feline order. Several of the felines backed away from the circle and sprinted toward the homestead. They'd return dressed and with rope to secure the men until the cops arrived from Tekapo or Twizel.

Marsh sent a questioning yowl at Leo.

"He's coming around. Breathing is labored. I think he's winded. Looks as if he's broken his leg. Right front. Ricky, breathe. That's it. Slow and easy. He's all right, Marsh."

Marsh growled his displeasure, relief filling him when he heard a whimper from his son.

It seemed like ages, but it was only five minutes later when two of the farmhands arrived to take charge of the man Marsh was guarding.

Marsh growled at him and feinted a charge. The man screamed.

"Keep him away from me. He bit me."

"Lucky for you it wasn't worse," Gerald, a farmhand, snapped.

They marched him toward the cluster of men, leaving Marsh to reassure himself that Ricky was unharmed. He shifted and crouched beside Leo and Ricky. With gentle hands, he checked his son for other injuries.

"I wish we were closer to Middlemarch so Gavin could take a look at him," Marsh said. Gavin was the local vet and as a feline, he acted as doctor to the feline population.

"Isabella is experienced with field medicine," Leo said.

Marsh scooped up Ricky, and both men turned toward the homestead.

"What happened? How did Ricky get out here?"

"I'm not sure," Leo said. "Both Caroline and Ricky were outside and Ricky took after the men. I told Caroline to stay

201

and that I'd go after Ricky. I had him with me, and everything was all right until that guy ran in our direction. Ricky ran before I could grab him."

Marsh let out a soft curse. "What the hell am I going to do with him, Leo? I explain how to shift every day. Hell, I've even told him he won't be able to open his birthday presents if he stays in feline form. Nothing I say seems to get through to him."

"You should return to Middlemarch and see Gavin. Hamish would give you a few days off. Cam will be back soon. You don't want to return to Middlemarch, do you?"

"Hell, no. I'll talk with Caroline. See what she thinks we should do. I guess we could book into the Middlemarch bed and breakfast for a few days."

"Stay with Saber and Emily. They're finding it strange since we've all moved out. They won't mind for a few days. Have Caroline make Emily a new dress or something. Isabella tells me Caroline is a genius."

"I'll talk to Caroline," Marsh repeated. No way was he doing anything without input from his mate.

When they turned into the gravel driveway, Caroline ran to meet them.

"Marsh! Is he hurt?"

"Leo thinks he has a broken leg."

Caroline stood aside to usher them into the house. "Lay him on the kitchen table."

Ricky whimpered.

"How do we treat him?" Caroline demanded. "Should we try to get him to shift?"

Marsh wrapped his arm around her trembling shoulders. "He'll heal better in feline form. Isabella will be here soon. Leo said she has experience in field medicine."

"As an assassin?"

Leo looked startled. "She told you? She must like and trust you. Only the family knows the truth."

"Sorry. She didn't say it was a secret. I won't mention it to anyone else," Caroline said.

"Do you have clippers? We'll need to shave off some of his fur so we can see his leg," Leo said.

Caroline disappeared to get clippers while Marsh grabbed a pair of jeans.

Isabella arrived, guns still in hand. "I need to lock these up. How is he?"

"Broken leg. Who takes care of medical problems here at the station?" Leo asked.

"Maria and Cam, I think. Hamish will know," Marsh said.

Isabella surveyed Ricky's leg and examined him for other wounds. "We could ring Gavin now, ask him."

"Who is Gavin?" Caroline demanded.

"He's the vet at Middlemarch, and he takes care of any feline medical issues," Leo explained.

"I'll ring him now," Caroline said. "Do you have his number?"

Marsh watched his mate, pride filling him as she spoke with Gavin. She explained about Ricky, his age, his unexpected shift and his injuries.

"I can x-ray him here at the surgery. His feline genes will heal him, but it would be best if I can see the damage. If he heals with the bone out of line, he'll end up with a limp."

Caroline nodded. "Can we give him something for the pain?"

"Any head injuries?"

Caroline glanced at Ricky who lay unmoving on the table. "He seems more shocked than anything. He's awake and responds if we speak to him."

"I gave Maria and Cam some mild sedatives. Give him a quarter of a tablet if you can get him to take it. Give him water if he wants it, but don't give him any solid food in case I need to operate."

Marsh gripped Caroline's arm as she went pale.

"All right," she whispered. "Thank you. We'll see you in a few hours." She hung up and handed the phone back to Leo. "He said—"

"We all heard, kitten," Marsh said in a gentle tone. "I'll pack a bag for us."

"What about James?" Caroline asked.

"I'll ring Dara and ask if she'll look after him for a few days." Marsh picked up the phone and dialed. After a quick conversation, they'd organized James. Dara's mate arrived shortly after to collect their oldest son.

Leo contacted Hamish, and half an hour later, they were in Leo's vehicle and on their way to Middlemarch.

Caroline sought his hand in the darkness of the rear of the vehicle. "I think we should see your parents while we're in Middlemarch. Once we're sure Ricky is okay, we'll visit them together. They'll want to know about Ricky."

Surprise at her compassion filled Marsh. His parents had treated her badly, and yet her first thought was for them because she knew they loved their grandchildren.

"It won't hurt them to know that our marriage is strong again, that we're mates," Caroline added.

Marsh heard a soft chuckle from Isabella and smiled himself. He liked the way Caroline thought. It wouldn't hurt his parents to learn they'd been wrong.

They'd left Middlemarch mere weeks ago, yet it felt as if it had been much longer. Caroline eyed the familiar Rock and Pillar range, the piles of schist that always reminded her of discarded children's Lego blocks and the green paddocks. Even in the muted light of early morning, the green of the Strath Tarei valley contrasted with the brown tussock of the Mackenzie. The stock were different too, the sheep much whiter since they weren't the merino breed that always looked as if they needed a good bath.

"Gavin is expecting us," Leo said. "We'll go to his place to sort out Ricky, then I'll take you out to the farm."

"Thanks," Marsh said.

Caroline nodded, tired but concerned about Ricky. At least he'd slept for most of the rapid journey. Leo had driven fast but with competence.

He drove into the township, took a right and pulled up in front of a wooden house on a large section. The front light flicked on as soon as Leo switched off the ignition, but she was the only one who required the illumination. A tall man with a mass of black curls, a worn T-shirt stretched over his chest and jeans with holes. They were almost white from many washings, but she got the impression the holes were by accident rather than design.

"Bring him into the surgery," the man ordered.

Marsh climbed from Leo's SUV and scooped Ricky off the rear seat. Caroline followed her mate into the surgery. She'd expected Leo and Isabella to drive home since it had been such a long night, but they crowded into the surgery too.

"Gavin, you know Marsh," Isabella said. "This is his mate Caroline."

Gavin nodded and indicated that Marsh should place Ricky on the examination table. "He's only three?"

"Yes," Caroline said.

"Is he eating normally?"

"Yes, he has a good appetite."

Gavin smiled at Caroline. "You're doing a good job. He's in excellent condition. I know this can't be easy for you."

His manner and the careful yet skilled way he examined Ricky put her at ease.

"Ah, I see the problem with his leg. It's a low break and we can put a splint on easily enough." He prodded with care, and Ricky woke up with a snarl. Gavin stroked his head and spoke to him in a soothing voice. "I'm the doctor, Ricky. We're going to fix your leg for you." Gavin spoke to them again. "I'll take an x-ray, but I'm confident it's a simple fracture. He should heal in a few weeks."

Caroline clutched Marsh, relief so instant that dizziness assailed her. She wavered on her feet and leaned into Marsh when he slid his arm around her waist.

"Thank you. Ricky is never sick. He had the normal booster shots— I didn't think to ask. Do the immunization shots hurt felines? They didn't seem to worry either of the boys. Should the doctor have noticed anything different at birth?"

"No, the feline genes are present if the doctor knows what to look for, but the changes that mark our blood work as different kick in when we shift for the first time," Gavin said.

"So Ricky can't see a human doctor now."

"I'm afraid he's stuck with me," Gavin said with a grin. "Okay, Ricky. I'm going to take a picture of your leg, so I can see the bones inside. Would you like to see?"

Ricky nodded.

Gavin scooped him up and carted him across the surgery. "You need to stay still. Can you do that for me?"

Ricky gave a yowl of assent.

"I'm thinking we'll give you a bright yellow cast, so your mother can see you in the dark. How does yellow sound?"

Ricky turned his head to look at her, and Caroline could have sworn he grinned.

The entire process didn't take long and Ricky soon sported a sunshine-yellow cast on his right front leg.

"Leo, would you mind taking Ricky out to the vehicle?" Marsh asked. "I want to have a quick word with Gavin."

"No problem." Leo picked up Ricky and carried him from the surgery. Isabella hesitated, then followed.

"Any suggestions on how to get Ricky to shift?" Caroline asked.

"He's healthy. He has a few tender spots from his fall, but his feline genes will heal the bruises in a few days. His break will also heal fast. I'm afraid all you can do is make sure he knows the shifting process and wait until he wants to shift. None of us can force him, and the more you growl or chastise him, the harder he'll dig in his heels. The problem is he likes being a cat, and he's too young to realize he can have both forms. For him, it's either cat or human, and he's having more fun living in his feline skin. I'll give you vitamins. You have an older son too?"

"Yes," Marsh said.

"I'll give you enough for both boys. You're already doing a great job with his diet and exercise. He'll shift when he has a powerful enough reason. It might be something as simple as opening a birthday or Christmas present or going on an excursion where he needs to be in human form. I know you must be worried, but physically, there is nothing wrong with him."

"Thank you." Caroline leaned against Marsh. "You've put my mind at rest. I-I thought it might be something I'd done."

"No." Gavin smiled, and it took his austere face to handsome. "I'm only a phone call away. A helicopter ride in an emergency."

"What happens if he tries to shift while he has his cast on?"

"He'll break it, and you'll have to come back for another one," Gavin said.

Caroline frowned. "Oh, dear."

"It's not a problem," Gavin reassured her.

"Thanks." Caroline turned to leave but Marsh stayed her.

"One more thing, Gavin. Can we get birth control for Caroline?"

Caroline gaped at Marsh, her cheeks heating.

Gavin smiled again. "You're mates?"

"Yes," Marsh said.

"Let me take your blood pressure and ask a few questions, Caroline." He was competent and thorough, asking what she was using now.

"I haven't taken one today. In the rush, I forgot."

"Perfect," Gavin said. "I can give you a shot. It will last for six months, and I'll give you a reminder when you require the booster."

"Is it safe for me?"

"Emily comes here if that's any help," Gavin said. "When Marsh marked you, he added feline enzymes to your blood. Now that you have those, you fall into the strange category, and we don't want humans studying your blood."

"I thought I'd received the pertinent information," she said with a glance at Marsh.

"Sorry," he said, his gaze watchful. Cautious. "It's been crazy since we moved to Glenshee."

"But not boring," she said.

The anxiety cleared from his expression. "No, never boring."

"You can ring me any time," Gavin said. "Preferably not at two in the morning, but during the day." He took care of the shot and placed a bright green plaster over the spot.

Caroline noticed he had a selection of bright colors, and he saw her interest.

"I like color," he said. "I have to wear conservative clothes so I don't attract attention, but you should see my underwear."

"That's true," Marsh said with a snort. "Have you not noticed the animals of Middlemarch sport bright collars and brands?"

"I hadn't, but I'll be looking now. Thanks, Gavin. How much do we owe you?"

Marsh took care of the payment, and Caroline waited until he'd finished. It was so good to have money again, to see the pride in which Marsh paid their medical charges. Small things, but they made her happy too.

"You must be exhausted," Emily said as she ushered them into the house.

"I'm hungry," Isabella announced.

"You're always hungry," Caroline said. "If I ate half the food you eat, I'd be the size of a bus."

"A very sexy bus," Marsh said and he kissed her, a quick press of lips that sent a zip through her body. Ricky wriggled and Marsh set him on the floor.

"I'm off to the café, but I've left food for you." She smiled as Ricky yawned, displaying a set of sharp teeth. "I'll show you your rooms. Ricky, do you want to see your room?"

He made a sound halfway between a grunt and a yowl and hobbled after Emily.

"I want to pick him up," Caroline said after she had settled Ricky and returned to the kitchen.

"He needs to exercise," Leo said. "He'll get the hang of the cast."

"When are we going to see your parents?" Caroline asked.

"I need sleep first," Marsh said. "I want a clear head when we visit them."

"Let me know when and you can borrow a vehicle," Leo said.

Caroline glanced at Marsh. "This afternoon? If we leave it any longer, gossip will get to them before we can drop by at the farm."

"Gavin won't talk and neither will we," Isabella said. "I didn't see any vehicles, so I doubt anyone saw us."

"Isabella would know," Emily said. "She notices everything. I'll see you later. Help yourself to food and call me at the café if you need anything."

Caroline hugged Emily, tears of appreciation blurring her vision. "Thank you." She was so lucky she'd met the Mitchells. Every one of them.

Isabella and Leo left too with instructions to ring them when they were ready to drive to visit Marsh's parents.

Caroline poured them another cup of coffee, then she and Marsh cleaned the kitchen and did the dishes.

"I'm ready for bed." Marsh tugged her from the kitchen and down the passage to their allocated bedroom. He turned to her a sexy glint in his green eyes. "Are you too tired to make love?"

"I could do that." Caroline kept her tone airy, making Marsh grin.

"Good. Two reasons why we shouldn't go to sleep straight away. I want you and if we make love, our scents will combine more. It's good for my parents to know that we're mates in all ways."

"*Eew!*" Caroline wrinkled her nose.

"Forget my parents," Marsh ordered. "We're the important ones. Our family."

"Yes."

Their gazes met and suddenly they were both flinging off their clothes.

"Wait," Caroline said. "We'd better check on Ricky."

"I'll go," Marsh said, and he slipped from the bedroom, not bothering to grab any clothes to screen his nakedness.

A sin to cover that backside. Caroline smiled and picked up their clothes, laying them over the back of a chair. She liked the way they looked mixed together.

"He's sound asleep. I'll leave the door ajar. He'll come and find us if he needs something."

"As long as he doesn't walk in on us in the middle—"

Marsh lifted her off her feet and swung her onto the bed. "I'll hear him, especially with the cast. Any other objections to getting busy?"

"Not a one."

Marsh joined her on the bed and claimed her mouth as if he meant business. She melted into his embrace, savoring his easy strength and the hard muscles rubbing against her breasts. Just a touch—his touch—pushed her into need. His fingers strummed over her mark, and she moaned, the sound trapped between their lips.

Caroline clung to him, kissing his mouth, his neck. She bit his marking site, and he froze, his groan of pleasure one of the sexiest things she'd ever heard.

She bit a fraction harder and broke the skin. The coppery taste of blood should have repelled her, yet strangely, it didn't.

Marsh groaned again, and she released her grip. "Lick it," he said in a thick voice.

213

Her tongue lashed out, and he parted her legs. He positioned himself and pushed inside her, filling her with a single thrust.

His mouth fastened over her mark as he thrust. As always, his touch pushed her hard and high. She kissed the spot where she'd bitten him and his strokes quickened. Up. Up. Up. Her orgasm was quick and powerful, a release of tension. An expression of their love.

He climaxed not long after her, his big body shuddering.

"I love you, Caroline. So much." Marsh's voice shimmered with emotion.

She cupped his face and stared deep into his sexy eyes. "I love you too. I am so glad we've worked out our problems."

Marsh kissed her lips and laughed. "Now we have an entirely new set."

"It doesn't matter. We'll face them together."

"I'm sorry I didn't tell you everything earlier."

"You should have," she agreed. "But you were trying to do the right thing. I should have done things differently too. Talked about our problems instead of hiding my head in the sand."

"We've both learned. Grown." Marsh yawned. "I'm tired."

"Me too."

"Maybe if we sleep long enough we can put off my parents until tomorrow."

Caroline laughed. "No more hiding, remember?"

"Yes, kitten."

She fell asleep with a smile on her face.

Chapter 13

Togetherness

It was late afternoon when they set out to visit Marsh's parents.

"I'm nervous," Caroline confessed, glancing across at Marsh.

"Me too," he admitted. "But mostly I feel ashamed."

Her brows knit together as she struggled to understand. "About what?"

"The way I let them dictate my behavior. I should have trusted my gut from the start."

"We both made mistakes," Caroline said. "The main thing is that we've corrected them and we know where we're heading now."

"To face off with my parents?"

"No, silly. With our relationship. I am happy. I enjoy living and working at the station. The kids enjoy it too."

"I like working for Cam. The other men work hard and make me feel like part of the team. There's no pettiness or rivalry or any of that shit."

She smiled, her happiness bleeding into a visual portrayal of a smile. "So, we're on the same page. About everything."

Marsh reached for her hand and squeezed. "Yes."

"Your neck," she blurted, noticing the faint raised scar, a match for hers.

His expression held pleasure as he lifted her fingers to the mark. His skin radiated warmth beneath her fingers. "I was wondering how long it would take you to notice."

"I did that?"

"You did." Lazy satisfaction coated his voice. "That doesn't happen with most human-feline pairings. It means we're meant to be together. True mates."

"Really?" Amazement. Delight. Desire. The differing emotions struck her like gunfire. Love. How had she ever thought she could walk away from this amazing man? Her mate.

"Really." He slowed Leo's SUV, then stopped behind a bus, which blocked the road.

Caroline craned her neck, watched a group of women—teenagers—pile off the bus. "What are they doing?"

"This must be the padlock fence everyone is discussing."

"Um...that doesn't look like a padlock."

"No." Marsh barked out a laugh. "It's not. Should I dare you to—"

"No, you should not. Bras are expensive and we can't afford to replace mine," she said in a prim voice.

"But we will be able to afford sexy lingerie," he said, his gaze on the increasing number of bras attached to the fence.

Caroline shook her head and grinned as the women laughed and cackled like cartoon hyenas, clutching each other as they piled back onto the bus. Finally, the bus driver moved off, no longer halting their progress.

"I heard a rumor that the Feline council doesn't approve of the lingerie decorating their fence," Marsh said as they drove past.

"Who is on the council? Are you allowed to tell me?"

"You're one of us now," Marsh said and told her.

Caroline pictured the women and wrinkled her nose. "I can't see Agnes Paisley and Valerie McClintock approving of young women displaying their underwear. I used to see them at school functions. They scared me."

"They scare me too. Saber mentioned they have someone clear the fence most weeks." He glanced at his watch as he pulled into the driveway. "I don't know if Dad will be at home."

"Doesn't matter. It's your mother I need to speak with." She squared her shoulders and willed away her nerves. This wouldn't be easy. She knew that, but she also realized she had to do this for peace of mind. She'd let her in-laws walk all over her. No longer. She was with Marsh for the long haul, and they needed to give her respect. Marsh deserved their respect too since he'd put up with a load of crap from his parents.

"Looks as if Dad is at home," Marsh said in surprise.

"It's best if we speak with them both at the same time."

He halted the vehicle and switched off the ignition. Marsh squeezed her knee and smiled in encouragement. "We'll give them a united front."

"Yes." Caroline climbed from the car and wiped her palms on her denim skirt. Her in-laws would smell her fear. Too bad.

The front door to the house opened and her mother-in-law stood in the doorway.

Her lips twisted. "Well, look what the cat dragged home."

Marsh watched Caroline lift her chin and stare down his mother.

"Is Charles at home?" Caroline asked, her voice cool.

Surprise flashed across his mother's face, and that didn't happen often. "Yes, he came home to get more staples. They'd run out. He's having something to eat before he heads out again."

"Good. Marsh and I would like to speak with you both."

"If you think we're going—"

"Mum," Marsh said, slipping his hand around Caroline's waist. She trembled, and that pissed him off. "Where is he? In the kitchen?"

"In the dining room."

Marsh ushered Caroline toward the dining room.

"If you've come back to ask for your job," his father said.

"We had to bring Ricky to see Gavin," Marsh said, keeping his voice even.

"You told her," his mother said.

"I'm Marsh's wife." Caroline focused on his parents. "Why shouldn't he tell me?"

"Don't mean nothing," Charles said and returned to his meal.

"I'm his mate." Caroline stood tall, and Marsh was proud of her.

Dawn snorted. "You don't know what you mean."

Caroline tugged aside the collar of her blouse to display her mark. "I am Marsh's mate."

"She's a human," Charles spat, tossing down his knife and fork. They clattered on the plate and splattered tomato sauce over the cream tablecloth.

"Caroline is my chosen mate." Marsh's tone hit strident.

"We came to tell you I am aware of the feline community. Marsh and I are mates. There was something else," she said. "Ricky shifted to feline. He—"

"Rubbish," Dawn said. "Why would you tell us such lies?"

Marsh scowled at his mother, wondering if they'd ever loved him. Their behavior was inexcusable. "It's true, and there is no need to be rude to Caroline."

"She's a human," Charles scoffed.

"I am Marsh's mate and mother to your grandchildren. Feline children, of which one has shifted already." She stomped over to the phone that sat on the far end of the table and carried it back to thrust at his mother. "Ring Gavin. Ask him if you won't believe me."

"We are true mates, Mother," Marsh said and shoved aside the collar he'd arranged to hide his mark. He took satisfaction in the way his mother's mouth gaped. "Which isn't the case with you and Dad."

"You're James and Ricky's grandparents, and I know you love them, no matter what you think of me," Caroline said. "I thought you should know about Ricky. He has a broken leg."

"A broken leg?" Dawn frowned at the mark on his neck.

"An accident," Marsh said. "It's a clean break, and Gavin says it will heal."

"Where are you living?" Charles asked.

Marsh knew what his father was asking but pretended to misunderstand. "We're staying with Saber and Emily."

"Another human," his father spat.

"Also happy and mates," Caroline said with a sweet smile. "Your prejudice is showing."

"That's enough," Marsh said.

Caroline placed her hand on his shoulder just as he was about to tell his parents exactly what he thought. "Marsh and I are happy. Our marriage is strong and our sons are enjoying their new home. Ricky and James would like to keep in contact, but neither Marsh nor I will put up with you spouting poison in their ears about humans. I have no idea why you hate me so much or why you're so horrible to your son. We have no intention of allowing you to spread your prejudices to our sons.

It's up to you how this goes. You behave with decency and treat me as part of the family or you have no contact with your grandchildren."

"That's blackmail," Dawn said with a gasp. "You can't do this. I'll appeal to the council."

"You're not fit to bring up our grandchildren," Charles snapped.

"You appeal to the council," Marsh said, angry at his parents. He'd tried so hard over the years, put up with their rudeness, their lack of affection, their slights to his mate. Hell, he'd even gone along with their edict, and that had almost destroyed his marriage. "The council will side with us."

"You will only look stupid. We're good parents," Caroline added.

His parents wouldn't change. "Let's go." He propelled Caroline from the house.

"I thought we could work things out." Caroline glanced at him. "I've made things worse."

"We did the right thing," Marsh said, twining their fingers together. "Don't worry, kitten. This is on my parents. We have done nothing wrong."

"But—"

He pressed his fingers over her lips. "No, enough. Guilt kept me persisting, but it's time. If they want to cling to their bitterness, let them. We don't have to dance to their tune any longer. We've moved on and so should they. Okay?"

SHELLEY MUNRO

"You're right," she conceded when he moved his fingers. "What should we do for the rest of the afternoon?"

"Let's go for a coffee, then I have another idea of a way to fill in time."

"But Leo is looking after Ricky."

"He told me to take my time. He said he owed you because you'd helped Isabella."

"Me?"

"Something about helping her find a new direction."

"Oh." Caroline climbed into the vehicle. "Isabella is changing my life by investing in material and selling the things I make at the craft fair."

Marsh grinned. "If it earns us free babysitting, I'm in favor."

"I suggested she hold martial arts classes for the kids and self-defense classes for the adults."

Marsh started the SUV and backed up.

"Marsh."

He glanced at her then saw his mother running toward them. His father came outside and stopped just outside the doorway. He wound down his window.

"Marsh, I'm sorry. You're right. We want to see our grandchildren. Are...are you staying in Middlemarch?"

"No, we're leaving as soon as we're sure Ricky is okay. Probably tomorrow."

"Can we see the children?"

"James isn't with us. He stayed at Glenshee Station."

"You're working for Cam Sinclair?"

"Yes," Marsh said.

"Can I see Ricky?"

Caroline leaned toward Marsh so she could see Dawn. "Ring us at Saber's. We'll arrange a time for you to visit before we leave. He'll be excited to see you."

"Thank you, Caroline. I-I appreciate that." His mother sounded subdued. She nodded and retreated to join her husband.

Marsh navigated the driveway and pulled out onto the main road. "That was well done of you."

"The boys love them. Your parents are good with them. They'll come 'round and accept me one day."

And maybe pigs would fly over Glenshee and perform acrobatics for all to see. "Maybe," he said.

When they arrived at the café, they joined Emily and Saber for a late lunch. Saber left to meet Felix, and Emily to cook a birthday cake while he and Caroline had a second cup of coffee. Once they'd finished, Marsh went to see Tomasine who was working the counter. He purchased a cupcake for Ricky and spotted something else. Ah.

"We have special paint you can use to personalize your padlock," Tomasine said. "We don't lend it to visitors. You're special."

"Thanks." Marsh winked at her while he thought quickly. Although his first instinct was to make it a surprise, Caroline was the artist in the family. "That would be great."

He accepted the box of paints and brushes and his cupcake and went back to the table. "I thought we'd put our own padlock on the fence to celebrate second chances."

Caroline beamed at him. "That's a wonderful idea."

"Tomasine gave me some paints." He handed her a paintbrush. "You're the artist."

"What should I paint?"

"How about our names and the date of our wedding?"

"Okay." With delicate strokes of the brush, she wrote their names—Caroline and Marsh—plus the date of their wedding. Then, once the paint dried, she turned over the padlock and painted a tiny stick figure with red hair.

Marsh smiled at her, the concentration on her face and the tip of her tongue visible between her lips. By the time she finished, a tiny black cat sat on its haunches beside the figure.

"What do you think?"

"Perfect," Marsh said with approval. "Let's clip it to the fence."

After returning the paints to Tomasine, they walked hand-in-hand to the SUV.

"Are you worried about Ricky?" Caroline asked. "Do you think he'll shift back to human?"

"I think Ricky will be fine." Marsh said. "Once he realizes, he can't leave Glenshee Station as much, I think he'll be more amenable to returning to his human form. Hamish told me they hold a mid-year Christmas. Ricky loves Christmas."

Caroline nodded. "I didn't think Gavin seemed worried, even though Ricky's early change is unusual. That set my mind at rest. I liked him."

"We're lucky to have him. Most communities have to make do."

"Are there other shifters living nearby?"

"No, but there are several communities in Australia."

"What about werewolves and vampires? Dragons?"

"There are a few werewolves around, but no groups in New Zealand as far as I know. I haven't heard of vampires, but we have native dragons. The taniwha."

"I thought they were legends."

Marsh pulled up near the fence, glad they were the sole visitors at present. "Think again."

"Wow." Her lashes blinked. Once. Twice. "That is amazing. Do the dragons fly?"

"Some of them."

"Wow."

"Come on, kitten. Let's hang our padlock before another bus or carload of ladies come to leave their bras."

Dozens of padlocks filled the five-wire fence, each one decorated in a different style and color.

"Where should we put our padlock?"

"There," Caroline said, her smile sweet. Sexy.

"I love you, kitten. Thank you for giving us a second chance." He slipped the top of their padlock on the wire and clipped it shut.

"Marsh, I'm so happy. I love you too."

He wrapped his arms around her and kissed her and not even the rude tooting of the horn from a newly arrived vehicle pulled them from the special moment.

This truly was love, and he was a lucky, lucky man.

Chapter 14

Bonus Chapter

Mitchell Farm, Middlemarch, New Zealand

Feline Shapeshifter Council Meeting.

Present: Saber Mitchell, Sid Blackburn, Kenneth Nesbitt, Agnes Paisley, Valerie McClintock, Benjamin Urquart

"There is no point glaring at me." Saber Mitchell glanced around the table at his fellow Feline council members, determined not to buckle under the silent condemnation. "You told me to speak with Marsh. I was following orders."

Valerie sniffed. "You arranged a new job for Marsh Rutherford."

Saber rolled his eyes, a habit he'd acquired from Emily, his mate. It made him want to smile, but he kept his expression under control. Not the right moment. If he let the oldies push him too far, he'd never regain the lost ground. At least he had a backup distraction in hand, although he wasn't desperate yet. "Let's speak plainly, shall we? Not one of you wanted to speak with Marsh or interfere in another man's marriage, so you delegated the job to me. I spoke with Marsh, discerned the problem and gave him the means to take steps for change. He wanted that change or he wouldn't have followed my suggestion."

"Dawn and Charles Rutherford aren't happy," Agnes said.

"When are they happy? They're miserable people, and they wanted to control their son. From the little I've pieced together, Charles used him as slave labor and refused to pay him a decent wage. They made their disapproval of Caroline clear."

Sid ran his hand through his thin silver hair, his sigh heavy. "They blamed him for his older brother's death. It was an accident, but Angus was the golden child. His passing was a bad day for Middlemarch."

"Marsh shouldn't keep paying for an accident," Kenneth stated. "He wasn't much more than a boy. Hadn't been shifting for that long."

"Is it true that one of Marsh's sons shifted?" Ben demanded.

"Yes. He's three."

"That could be a problem," Agnes said with a scowl. "No wonder Dawn and Charles want custody of their grandchildren."

"That will happen over my dead body," Saber stated. "But from what Marsh said, his parents are starting to come around and have backed off on their threats. They have no grounds. Marsh and Caroline are good parents, and the boys are doing well at Glenshee Station. It's a secluded property, so his feline appearance won't startle anyone." He met each of their gazes. "Gavin isn't concerned, says the boy is in excellent health and he'll shift back to human when he's ready. The only way Dawn and Charles will have contact with their grandchildren is with Marsh and Caroline's permission. Are we clear?"

Silence bloomed before Kenneth beamed at Saber. "Sounded just like Herbert then. Lord, I miss that man. He was a force."

Saber opened and closed his mouth. He missed his uncle too. "Are we agreed? There will be no more interference in Marsh and Caroline's marriage. They are happy—ecstatically," Saber said, recalling the noise from the spare bedroom before they returned to Glenshee. "They are also mates. True mates," he added, recalling seeing the mark on Marsh's neck. The same mark he sported after Emily had bitten him during lovemaking. He hadn't known that would or could occur, but he wore the mark with pride.

"The lad is right," Sid said. "He dealt with the problem as he saw fit. I, for one, will stand by his actions. I spotted Marsh and Caroline at the padlock fence as I drove past. They were lost in each other, and it made an old heart proud." He grinned. "A carload of young girls came and were hooting and hollering, but Marsh and Caroline didn't seem to notice."

"Did they leave bras?" Valerie demanded.

"I can't say," Sid said. "I was in a hurry." He turned his head and winked at Saber.

"What is next on the agenda?" Saber asked.

"Isabella, your sister-in-law, has put forward a proposal to run martial arts classes for children and teenagers plus keep-fit and self-defense classes for adults," Agnes said. "She says she's happy to donate the proceeds, after expenses, to the council. What angle is she playing? Why is she donating her profits?"

Saber knew but wasn't about to tell the council they had a professional assassin—albeit retired—living in their midst. "She is independently wealthy," Saber said. "Her parents left her a large amount of money, and she doesn't need to work." The truth as far as it went.

"Well," Valerie said. "She doesn't behave like a rich person."

"I say we should approve her proposal," Sid said. "The more we have to occupy our youngsters, the better it will be for everyone. If we'd had something like this ten years ago..." He trailed off, which Saber was grateful for. He did not want reminders of his rambunctious brothers.

"I think it would be a good thing," Saber said. "Isabella is a good teacher. She's been running through her program with me and Emily plus Tomasine and Felix. She is also teaching Sylvie."

"I agree," Kenneth said and wiped his sweaty brow.

The rest added their approval.

"One last thing. Leo, Felix and I have completed building the zombie run course. I suggest I take you for a tour of the course and show you the obstacles, the places the zombies will inhabit and the running tracks."

"A tour," Valerie said, doubt coloring her voice.

"You're on the council," Saber said. "You've all been closely involved with our other functions and gatherings. This one shouldn't be any different."

"I'm wearing my good clothes," Agnes snapped.

"You can change. I suggest I take you all around the course in one hour. That will give everyone a chance to grab their old clothes and gumboots. That rain we had yesterday has made everything muddy."

"At least the forecast is good for next weekend," Ben said. "I checked."

"Well?" Saber asked, allowing his grin free.

"You are a scamp," Valerie chided. "Fine, but you will open gates and help me over fences."

Ben nodded. "I'm curious. Wouldn't mind trying out the obstacles."

"I'll go," Agnes said. "But I refuse to force this old body over obstacles. I shall observe."

"We need to organize volunteers to check off competitors as they go over the obstacles," Saber said.

SHELLEY MUNRO

"Where is that piece of paper you gave us with other jobs on the day?" Sid shuffled through a pile of papers in front of him. "Ah. I'd be happy to man an obstacle. Should be fun."

"I'd like to see these zombies in action," Valerie said.

"We need zombie observers too. If you come around the course now, you can have first choice of the volunteer jobs," Saber said.

"One hour, you say?" Agnes stood. "Where do you want to meet?"

"At the gate on Mitchell Road," Saber said.

The council members hurried off, apart from Sid who remained seated since he was already in farm clothes. Kenneth and Ben had attended an auction in a neighboring town and were wearing their good clothes.

"You did well with the Rutherford problem, lad," Sid said. "I'm proud of you."

"Thanks. I didn't know Marsh well since he's younger than me, but I like him. Caroline has become friends with Emily, Tomasine and Isabella. They're a good match and deserve a chance."

"Charles Rutherford is a bitter old man. Always been that way. Why were you grinning?"

"I'm trying to imagine Valerie and Agnes on the zombie course. It is muddy. It's possible they'll fall on their butts."

"I see," Sid said, and his green eyes glittered with shared laughter. "It's just as well they're feline women and not easily damaged then."

232

Saber laughed out loud. "I should take my camera."

"At your peril, lad. At your peril."

And laughing, they walked from the house together to join the others at the zombie run course. It was a good day.

Thank you for reading MY ESTRANGED LOVER! The zombie run was a big topic of conversation at the latest council meeting, and the actual race takes place in the next book in the Middlemarch Shifters series, MY FELINE PROTECTOR.

Despite the council's careful planning, not everything goes smoothly...

Get your copy of MY FELINE PROTECTOR today
www.shelleymunro.com/books/my-feline-protector/

About Author

USA Today bestselling author Shelley Munro lives in Auckland, the City of Sails, with her husband and a cheeky Jack Russell/mystery breed dog.

Typical New Zealanders, Shelley and her husband left home for their big OE soon after they married (translation of New Zealand speak - big overseas experience). A twelve-month-long adventure lengthened to six years of roaming the world. Enduring memories include being almost sat on by a mountain gorilla in Rwanda, lazing on white sandy beaches in India, whale watching in Alaska, searching for leprechauns in Ireland, and dealing with ghosts in an English pub.

While travel is still a big attraction, these days Shelley is most likely found in front of her computer following another love - that of writing stories of contemporary and paranormal romance and adventure. Other interests include watching rugby (strictly for research purposes), cycling, playing croquet and the ukelele, and curling up with an enjoyable book.

Visit Shelley at her Website
www.shelleymunro.com

Join Shelley's Newsletter www.shelleymunro.com/newsletter

Visit Shelley's Facebook page
www.facebook.com/ShelleyMunroAuthor

Follow Shelley at Bookbub
www.bookbub.com/authors/shelley-munro

Also By Shelley

Paranormal

Middlemarch Shifters
My Scarlet Woman
My Younger Lover
My Peeping Tom
My Assassin
My Estranged Lover
My Feline Protector
My Determined Suitor
My Cat Burglar
My Stray Cat
My Second Chance
My Plan B
My Cat Nap
My Romantic Tangle
My Blue Lady
My Twin Trouble
My Precious Gift

Middlemarch Gathering

My Highland Mate

My Highland Fling

Middlemarch Capture

Snared by Saber

Favored by Felix

Lost with Leo

Spellbound with Sly

Journey with Joe

Star-Crossed with Scarlett